Dead, Mr Mozart

DEAD,
MR MOZART

BERNARD BASTABLE

St. Martin's Press
New York

DEAD, MR. MOZART. Copyright © 1994 by Bernard Bastable. All
rights reserved. Printed in the United States of America. No part of
this book may be used or reproduced in any manner whatsoever
without written permission except in the case of brief quotations
embodied in critical articles or reviews. For information, address
St. Martin's Press, 175 Fifth Avenue, New York, N.Y. 10010.

Library of Congress Cataloging-in-Publication Data

Bastable, Bernard.
    Dead, Mr. Mozart / Bernard Bastable.
       p.   cm.
    ISBN 0-312-11771-X (hardcover)
    I. Title.   II. Title: Dead, Mister Mozart.
  PR6052.A665D35   1995
  823'.914—dc20   94-44485
                                           CIP

First published in the United States by St. Martin's Press

First U.S. Edition: April 1995
10 9 8 7 6 5 4 3 2 1

For
Richard Rodney Bennett
Another Musician in Exile

'I am an out-and-out Englishman'
(W.A. Mozart, the real one, in a letter to his father,
19 October 1782)

CHAPTER ONE
Masonic Funeral Music

I had hardly turned out of my apartment house in Henrietta Street and begun in the direction of the Strand when I was struck by something unusual: almost all the people I passed were in their soberest dress, and had on their faces expressions of more than the usual dyspeptic English melancholy. Mr Gibbs the Attorney was bustling past and, seeing my bewilderment, he stopped.

'It's the King,' he explained.

'Worse, Mr Gibbs?'

'Dead, Mr Mozart.'

And he hurried on to take some doubtless necessary legal cognizance of the new reign. I turned and regained my apartment, where I ransacked my cupboards for black and dun-coloured articles of apparel – no easy matter, for even at my age I am generally considered something of a dandy. My proceedings were regarded with mystification by Ann, my little servant maid, who I sometimes think is hardly better than an idiot.

'It's the King. He's dead,' I explained.

I think she thought I said 'Mr King' – manager of the Grand Theatre, with whom I have had many dealings, mostly unsatisfactory to me – for she merely said 'Well I never', and went on with her work with no particular empressement. I went out again, more suitably draped to face a nation in mourning.

The first acquaintance I met who wanted to talk was Lord Egremere, a one-time patron in whose debt I shall always be. We gave the handshake and he launched into the inevitable subject.

1

'Sad news,' he said.

'Sad indeed, My Lord,' I replied with suitable gravity. However Lord Egremere is a Whig, and I could be a little more honest with him than I could with a lord of Tory sympathies. 'And yet—' how to put the thought that must have been in everybody's mind?—'and yet for the royal sufferer, perhaps a happy release?'

'Perhaps you're right. Certainly he deserved rest at last. I believe there was never any diminution in the . . . symptoms. So now we have a new reign, eh?'

'A new reign, and yet not a new reign, you might say, Mr Lord.'

He nodded sagely.

'Agreed, agreed. Prinny does seem to have been around for an age. Perhaps the excitements of Waterloo and Paris make it seem so. But still, a new reign! A Coronation! Maybe some festivities for a war-weary nation.'

That idea was new to me.

'I had not thought of a Coronation,' I admitted. 'It's so long since there has been one.'

'Before you came among us, eh, Mr Mozart?'

'I should hardly have remembered even if I had been here,' I pointed out (I am perhaps becoming a little bit touchy about my age, and the length of time I have been in this benighted country). 'Being only four or five at the time. You don't think the new King will forswear a Coronation, as being inappropriate to the spirit of the age?'

Lord Egremere threw back his head and laughed.

'You little know Prinny if you can imagine that! An opportunity to dress up? Pomp, circumstance, with him the centre of it all? He'll revel in it. Anyway, why should he forswear it? Revolution defeated, the old Sovereigns restored – no, Prinny will have his show, whatever people feel. And perhaps he'll be right: it will do the nation a power of good if it's well done, and Prinny should ensure that it is . . . Could be something in it for you, Mr Mozart.'

'For me, My Lord? Hardly, as a Catholic. I'm sure if there is any commission for music going it will be given to an Anglican and an Englishman.'

He shook his head.

2

'Oh, I wasn't thinking of music for the Coronation. I was thinking of something for the theatre. Our music theatre has been in a deplorable state for many years now.'

'It would be impossible to disagree with that, My Lord.'

'Revive its glories. Write something wonderful for Prinny's jollifications. A fine stately piece. No – more to the point, a fine comedy. Something to cheer the nation's spirits after the long war.'

The idea appealed to me at once.

'I do have something already in mind, My Lord . . .'

'Splendid! Well, set to! Give us something to cheer us all up. I'm sure it will go like anything.'

And with a wave he went on his way. The Lord Egremere is long on ideas, short on specifics. How the opera is to be revived without a theatre, without a fine company, without the best Italian voices, he did not deign to suggest.

It must have been the purest coincidence, but it was not ten minutes later that I was conversing with Mr Brownlett the banker in St James's, and after the preliminaries, which by now were becoming second nature, and the handshake, which was too, he said:

'What we need for the new reign is a new opera.'

I cleared my throat modestly.

'Lord Egremere has just said the same.'

'You're the man for it. Something to express the nation's joy – after a suitable period of mourning, of course.'

'Of course.'

'What was that piece you wrote – full of catchy tunes and magic and popular stuff like that?'

'I think you mean *The Enchanted Violin*.'

'That's what we want. Something light.'

Something light! Only my most sublime music, my deepest thought, my finest exploration of the human condition! Clothed in the form of a burlesque such as John and Susan might enjoy on their evening off, but nevertheless music to take with me to the Judgment Seat. And Brownlett remembers it as 'something light'! I would not for all the world have the ears of a banker.

He registered at least my speechlessness.

3

'Too early to think of it now, of course. Naturally, with the poor old King only a few hours dead. You'll feel it particularly, won't you? He was such a benefactor of yours.'

A benefactor! A benefactor! I saluted his departing back and went on my way. Those damned fifty guineas! Those fatal fifty guineas! What they have to answer for! I have spent my life cursing those fifty guineas.

My revered father (may God have granted rest at last to his spirit) brought me to these islands in 1764. I was then – though I say it myself, who am the only one qualified to say it – the most musically talented 7-year-old musician the world had ever known. I, with Nannerl (I salute you in beautiful Salzburg, dear and fortunate sister!) played for the beau monde, played for the gentry, played for royalty. In particular I played for the young King George and his incessantly pregnant and incurably ugly queen, Charlotte. Over and over I played for them, expending for them the abundance of my juvenile fancy and proficiency. My rewards? Over and over, a purse of fifteen guineas. Good, my dear but perhaps over-deferential father would say: not wonderful, but good. Nannerl and I would look at each other, each of us somehow knowing that it was not good but stingy. But as I say my poor father was always inclined to take too roseate a view of the great and powerful.

Then, when I had been in London for some months, I played for their majesties again at Windsor Castle, played with unparalleled brilliance and feeling, a concert fit for Saint Cecilia herself. Fool that I was! Infant dolt! We were rewarded with a purse of fifty guineas.

I myself believe it was the result of a mishearing: the King's English was notoriously guttural and unclear. His Majesty's love of music was really nothing more than a fixation on Handel, his patronage of me in later years consisting of constant requests to re-orchestrate his oratorios for larger forces. One can have enough even of masterpieces. I have had enough, over the years, of the *Messiah*.

But that was it. The die was cast. On the strength of

4

those fifty guineas my father decided to stay on with my mother and the two of us in London. So I have grown old, rheumaticky and asthmatic in the foggy damp of England, who might have been well and happy in the beneficent climates of Salzburg or Vienna. I have spent a good part of my life writing trivial theatre music for footmen and shop-girls, condescended to by Court and Church alike – I, who would have been courted by my Emperor, wooed by Archbishops, the intimate of intellectuals and the aristocracy.

O, accursed, fatal fifty guineas!

I went on my way grumbling, as I have grumbled to myself a thousand – nay, a million – times before. When I finally reached the Haymarket and the Queen's Theatre I found Mr Popper pacing the length of his office at the back of the theatre, as usual a mixture of pomposity and naïvety. In honour of the day we indulged in the handshake (something I normally avoid with Mr Popper, who should not have been admitted to any Lodge, nor indeed any less elevated association of gentlemen).

'Ah, Mr Mozart – no doubt you've heard? Of course. Terrible news, terrible. A national tragedy.'

I speculated yet again how anyone could describe as a national tragedy the death of a man who had been off his head these past nine years, and who spent his more lucid moments playing the organ at Windsor Castle (very badly, I am reliably informed, and Handel, I am morally sure). As before I held my peace, and merely bowed my agreement.

'The theatre, of course, will have to be shut. As a token of the musical world's participation in the national grief.' He didn't look at me directly, but shot me a sideways glance from his piggy little eyes. 'I propose to remain closed for – three days!'

I cleared my throat.

'That will hardly be long enough, my dear sir. The funeral will take longer than that to organise. We can hardly reopen before the funeral, while the other theatres remain closed.'

He fumed, as I knew he would.

'Why should it take any time to arrange a funeral? The

5

event is hardly unexpected – or only so insofar as we had all forgotten about him. Who is there to mourn him? His children who hated him, his countrymen who ridiculed him? I'd have thought they'd have buried him "hugger-mugger" . . . Oh, very well, then: we remain closed until after the funeral.'

It was meant as a dismissal, but I remained.

'Your apt quotation from *Hamlet*—'

'Eh?'

'—reminds us that we should turn our thoughts to the new reign, and the new monarch.'

I had struck an immediate chord. There came into his eye a look of calculation. I had seen it so often I had at last learned to capitalise on it.

'You're right,' he said. 'We can't reopen until after the funeral because it would look disrespectful to the new King. Though in the circumstances it's hard to think of him as a *new* King.'

'I said the same to Lord Egremere. The Prince has been reigning so long in all but name. Still, there will – after a decent period – be celebrations . . . A Coronation.'

Mr Popper slapped his thigh.

'God dammit, you're right, Mr Mozart. And what you're saying is that we must be part of those celebrations.'

'Exactly.'

'Put on something a bit special. A capital idea! Revive the Italian opera after all these years. What should it be, then? A production of *Il Matrimonio Segreto*?'

I closed my eyes in distress.

'The first Coronation for sixty years could only be celebrated, surely, by a new work.'

'A *new* work! A new Italian opera. My, but that would be setting our sights high. I like the idea immensely – immeasurably – but who would we get to write the music?'

I coughed, this time so meaningfully that I managed to pierce his pompous self-preoccupation without further prompting. 'You, Mr Mozart? You have ambitions to write further Italian operas? Yet how long is it since you wrote a full scale comic piece? It was a comic piece you had in mind?'

'Oh yes. A Coronation could only be celebrated in the theatre *joyously*.'

'Precisely. That would bring the customers in. You say you have a subject in mind?'

'Yes, I do, though I am having a little trouble with the title: *Le Moglie Allegre di Windsor?* . . .'

He raised his eyebrows in an attempt at satire.

'It hardly slips easily off your tongue, Mr Mozart – let alone the tongue of an Englishman.'

'*Le Donne Allegre?*'

'Better, much better. The simpler the better, I always say. But that is a detail . . .'

I saw from his eyes that he was sliding off into a reverie, so I slid off into one of my own. How long, he had asked, since I had written a comic opera in Italian? How long indeed? Since the disappearance from these shores of my good friend (if far from *good* friend) da Ponte, chased abroad and to the unpromising cities of America by creditors. How often did I lecture my friend on the proper method of managing indebtedness! How often did I explain ways – subtle, ingenious, gentlemanly ways – of getting into debt in such a manner that one could get out with impunity and without paying! To no avail. And yet, how grateful must I be to God for his years in England, and the glorious pieces that we made together: *Le Nozze di Figaro; Don Giovanni; Così Fan Tutte* (this last quite unappreciated by the beef-witted British).

My librettist for the new piece is a sad come-down. He is an estimable man – one of liberal sentiments, a Venetian fleeing persecution by what he misguidedly calls the city's Austrian oppressors. But being persecuted is no sure sign of being talented. He can no more read Shakespeare than I can read Confucius, and he has no notion of compression, of reducing the numbers of characters and incidents – of, in short, producing an *opera*, and an Italian opera in especial. But we proceed, we jog on. But, oh Lorenzo! If but you could return, without a plague of bailiffs descending!

I emerged from my reverie to find that Popper was still in his, but was now beginning to share it – muttering, his eyes still fixed on a horizon well beyond the Haymarket.

'A Coronation opera season! A Season of Italian Opera to Celebrate the Coronation of King George IV ... A Glorious Opera Season to Honour our Glorious Sovereign ... No, the people would never stand for "Glorious", though he could have a bout of popularity if he played his cards right ... Mme Ardizzi and Mme Pizzicoli Honour These Shores to Celebrate the Coronation of King George IV ...'

His eyes might be fixed on a distant horizon, but the light of madness glinted in them. How well do I know that madness, how often have I seen it in theatre managers. The lure of an Italian opera season. Entice Mme X from Paris with the promise of mounting the opera that shows her powers to their greatest advantage. Invite Mme Y from Naples, dangling before her a production of the opera that shows *her* powers to the greatest advantage. Lure Mme Z out of retirement at Kew and a comfortable existence as the mistress of a Royal Duke with the promise ...

What is the upshot? One by one they arrive, with a caravan of luggage and a retinue of husbands, lovers and hangers-on. Each expresses surprise, bewilderment, shock, contempt, to find that other *prime donne* than themselves have also been engaged. Manager temporises on the subject of the new staging of the various favourite operas. Each lady presses, each lady's lovers press, her husband, even, presses. Rows, ructions, substitute singers, cancelled performances, outraged reports in *The Times* and the *Morning Post*, and in the end: bankruptcy. Oh, I've seen it all so often before!

'I think that's a wonderful idea,' I said.

'But would they come, eh? Would they come?'

'For a Coronation Season – with the eyes of all Europe and all its sovereigns on Great Britain? Of course they would come.'

'Dear God, I think you're right.'

'If the ladies you've named won't come, I hear great things of Mme Hubermann-Cortino in Vienna.'

'What is her speciality?'

8

'I believe it's *Iphigénie en Tauride*.'

'Hmmm – Gluck, ain't it? Gluck's never popular, not here, not anywhere. Not as *you* were once popular, Mr Mozart.'

I bowed complacently, hoping he wasn't confusing me with someone else.

'I remember as a boy,' he went on, 'how they were all singing that Turkish thing—'

'*The Ladies of the Harem*.'

'How did it go, now? "Long live Bacchus, may he prosper, Bacchus was a worthy man".'

A 64-year-old does not like the works of his nonage quoted back at him as if they were his masterpiece. Mr Popper's voice and tuning were in any case intolerable, and I cut in quickly:

'That was truly a wonderful success. I shall aim for something similar with my new piece.'

'*Will* you? With the *Donne* Whatsit? Do please, dear Mr Mozart.' He had not been so polite to me since the year of Trafalgar. 'And will there be parts for Mme Ardizzi and Mme Pizzicoli?'

'For them and several other ladies. And of course a wonderful role for a bass.'

'For a bass?'

'England is the country of bass singers. We must try to find one we can teach Italian to.'

'It begins to sound wonderful, like the turning of a new page. We shall need patrons, of course, and backers.'

'Have you thought of Lord Egremere? He is always most generous to musicians and musical enterprise.'

Mr Popper shook his head.

'Not with the present rural poverty and discontent in the South. And why would a Whig celebrate the Coronation of the new King? He ditched them and they despise him.'

'Then what about the Marquess of Hertford—'

'Husband of the King's—'

'—great friend. Yes. He has an ear.'

'Not always an *open-handed* gentleman,' said Mr Popper dubiously.

'Not always,' I agreed, remembering that I was moderately indebted to him. 'But someone who likes the feeling of being a patron – likes the respect accorded a benefactor. And he certainly appreciates good music. He subscribed to my last set of symphonies.'

'Hmm. Well, I shall use the period of closure to write letters. To the ladies and their managers, of course, but also to rich and aristocratic potential patrons.'

'Write them, my dear sir, but best not send them just yet – not those to the backers.'

'Why not? Oh yes: too soon, of course. The aristocracy will feel bound to be grief-stricken at the death of a King. You too, Mr Mozart. You must feel it more than most of us. He was a great benefactor of yours, wasn't he?'

Oh, those accursed fifty guineas! They seem to have entered folk history. But I did not contradict him. I withdrew, leaving my poison to do its work. Knowing what I do about the destructive power of a determination to present Italian opera, I suppose I should have felt guilty.

In fact I felt more elated than I had done in years.

CHAPTER TWO
A Little Night Music

So for the first few months of the new reign, while everybody was wondering what Prinny would do about this and that (and finding that as a rule he would do remarkably little), letters were flying to and from Italy, Vienna and Paris, as Mr Popper attempted to put together an opera company worthy of the name. I meanwhile went on in my usual way, writing music for *William and Susan, Alice and Frederick*, or perhaps *The Maid of Moscow* or *The Wizard of Wolverhampton* – whatever little piece I was occupied with for the Queen's Theatre. These I called my left-hand pieces: the airs were a sort of musical diarrhoea which flowed out without effort or involvement on my part. I never read the whole book, out of concern for my sanity, but merely got the sense of each of the airs and simple concerted pieces (not always easy, admittedly, granted the quality of the poets employed by Mr Popper) and let appropriate music flow out. The income from such burlesques, which I augmented by directing them regularly to keep the players and singers in trim, kept me in beefsteak and wine and the occasional pretty new waistcoat. With my right hand and the best part of my time I was composing real music: the symphony for the Royal Philharmonic Society which the good Mr Novello claimed was my 105th, and of course *Le Moglie Allegre di Windsor* or whatever I finally decided to call it.

Mention of waistcoats prompts me to note that mourning for the late King was put off with remarkable dispatch. A general feeling that he had in effect been dead

11

before he died led to all ranks of polite society resuming their normal dress before February was out. It was said that even at Court mourning was hardly more than token and there no doubt Prinny (a notably unfilial son) led the way. Things might have been different if the old Queen had been alive, but she had died of dyspepsia two years before.

It was of the Court that many people were thinking in those early months of 1820, for there was a general feeling that, now Prinny, as we still called him, was King there ought to be feasting, laughter, celebrations – in short that more money ought to flow from the direction of the Court into the outstretched hands of his (for the moment, and somewhat conditionally) loyal subjects. This was a feeling I emphatically shared. Thus it was with a lift of the heart that, one day in early summer, I took from the hand of my little maid a missive which had been delivered to the door by someone 'terrible grand', in her words. I saw at once that the coat of arms on the cover was the royal one. When I had cautiously torn it open I found that it was an invitation to play a concert of my own compositions before King and Court at the Pavilion at Brighton on the fifth of June. The invitation courteously invited me to stay the night.

So, the wheel had come full circle: as a child I had played for the new King George III, and as an old man I was to play for the new King George IV. Many men would have felt saddened by this but I must confess that the invitation gave me no sense of staleness or over-familiarity: playing before the Sovereign brought undoubted rewards in the shape of reputation, increased fees, and also in tradesmen's willingness to extend credit. Dear, necessary credit! It was of course absurd that this should be so, since an appearance at Court cost infinitely more in the purchase of suitable clothes, the redeeming from hock of jewellery etc etc, than it brought in in the way of emoluments. But such was the case, and I was not one to fail to take advantage of it. *Eccomi là!*

The fifth of June saw me in a carriage with superb coachmen, put at my disposal by the royal mews. It was already clear (I hoped) that things were to be done in the new reign in a quite different style than had been the case when poor old Farmer George was in full possession of his wits. It is true that when I arrived at the Pavilion (which, it occurred to me, would provide a splendid setting for my old piece *The Ladies of the Harem*) I was shown to a room in the outer and upper reaches of that tinsel extravaganza. It was explained that the clement summer and the new reign had resulted in exceptional numbers of the aristocracy joining the Court. Who was I, a mere artist, to jostle for a good room with the nobility? I must confess that hot water in abundance was brought, and I was asked to talk with an officer of the Court at five o'clock in the North Drawing Room. I went down with some anticipation, but also with the confidence of long (if not recent) experience of performing before royalty for a pittance.

'Ah, Mr Mozart!' said a grand, portly and gaudy personage when I was ushered in. He was not the Lord Chamberlain. That was Lord Hertford, with whom I was acquainted through certain pecuniary transactions already mentioned, and through the Benefice Lodge, of which he and I were both members. But Lord Hertford, I later learned, was busy with the King on vital and urgent business, and I had to make do with the Vice Chamberlain. He clapped me familiarly on the shoulder. 'So glad you could accede to His Majesty's *very special* request for a concert of your works.'

I bowed and muttered the usual stuff.

'Only too honoured by the request, My Lord.'

'Your acquaintance with the new King goes back many years, I believe?'

Oh yes, many years we went back, the child prodigy and the prodigal child! I remembered an ante-chamber to the concert room at St James's Palace, where the young prince, six years my junior, had thrown himself on me, punching and shouting 'Why should I have to listen to a common German piano-strummer?' and another when he had tried to ruin my hands by hitting them with all his strength with a ruler. Since he had probably been soundly whipped at the time I decided to let bygones be bygones.

13

'It does indeed. To the time when we were both children.'

'His Majesty has always been most musical. The present impoverished condition of opera in London is most distressing to him, as I'm sure it is to you . . . Ah, er, Mr Mozart, the King has a little favour to ask of you . . .'

'Yes, My Lord?' (Heart sinking. More play for no more pay.)

'Your concert, as you know, is to be this evening. I had you shown to the North Drawing Room because of the pianoforte.' He waved a plump, lordly hand in the direction of a Broadwood grand. 'For if you should wish to – to practice. But His Majesty also wondered, as a way of – of limbering up, as it were—' he made me sound like a prize-fighter, punching a bag before a contest—'if you would be willing to – to play during dinner. Pleasant music, as an aid to digestion. An excellent instrument has been placed in the Banqueting Room.'

He faded into silence. So that was it – I was to be reduced to a mere salon pianist, providing music *in the background*, music to guzzle and slurp and gossip and giggle to. I loathe the fashion of having music going on *behind*, while attention is really on something else. I call it mush-ick, because it reduces music to a pleasant mush in the back of the mind. I swallowed hard, and thought of royal patronage for the opera season at the Queen's, perhaps a royal visit to *Le Donne Giocose*.

'I would of course be happy to comply with His Majesty's wishes, My Lord,' I said.

He breathed a sigh of relief, said he would send a footman to me at half-past five, when the Court were seated at table, and waved his hand again in the direction of the Broadwood. I needed no second bidding, for I was the prey of emotions which I was in the habit of working out of my system at the keyboard. I sat down and played the most aggressive thing I could think of – the first movement of a sonata by my good (but loud) friend, Herr Beethoven. That was what I would like to do to them!

It was about twenty minutes later, when I had modulated to more peaceful feelings and was playing the

14

andante of a sonata of my own – very delicate, peaceful music – that I suddenly became conscious that I was not alone in the room. I cast a look behind me and saw it was a woman listening. She gestured me to continue, but a minute or two later came over and leant over me at the keyboard. I recognised her now: a no-longer-young woman of full figure and somewhat equine features, very grandly dressed but trying (the effort showed) to unbend, to bring herself down to my level. It was someone I had *seen* before, but never spoken to: Lady Hertford, wife of one of the potential sponsors of the opera season and the . . . good friend of His Majesty King George IV.

'So beautiful. One of your own, I believe, Mr Mozart?'

'Indeed it is, My Lady. Composed last year.'

'You will be playing it tonight?'

'I had thought to, My Lady.'

'So much more suitable than the energetic Mr Beethoven, whom you were playing before.' She was now leaning forward, making me very conscious of her *décolleté* gown, and what it was largely failing to conceal. 'And I believe you have consented to play during dinner?'

'His Majesty was so kind as to ask me . . .'

'I'm sure you will judge admirably what would be most suitable. One would hardly want Mr Beethoven with one of the fish courses. People get uneasy if the music is too loud, and the good German is such a hammerer, is he not? As if the Day of Judgment were always just around the corner. I feel that anything grand or stately is hardly suitable for a meal. On the other hand a little pianissimo is always sure to please.'

She seemed to say it meaningfully, and a dreadful conviction gripped me. She was trying to seduce me! This horse-faced matron was giving me an *invitation* – me, who have remained chaste since my dear Connie died (except for Mrs Sackville in Frith Street for my absolute physical needs). She was even contrasting – was that it? – the stately and tedious lovemaking of her weighty royal protector with the gentle love-making she might hope for from me! I, a poor musician, was being *propositioned* by this enormously wealthy lady with a grand mansion near Leeds (a dirty, disagreeable town, my son Charles Thomas tells me, but very musical). And she was old enough to be my elder sister. Every reply I could think of seemed to contain a double meaning.

'I will remember Your Ladyship's advice,' I finally said. A gong sounded. She nodded and glided from the room.

I will pass quickly over events of the next few hours. I was summoned by a footman, who murmured that there would be dinner for me later (leftovers, no doubt, but I consoled myself with the thought that leftovers from a royal table would be very much better than anything I was accustomed to dine on in the normal way). As the brilliant assembly (to adopt the phraseology of the newspapers) progressed towards the Banqueting Hall from the Corridor the footman and I waited down the far end. As the last members of the Court took their places at table we too progressed forward and waited by the doorway. My eye went involuntarily up to the ceiling, to the magnificent chandelier with Chinese dragons, surmounted by sinister-looking exotic foliage which would not be out of place in my opera *The Enchanted Violin*. At last the lords and ladies were settled, grace was said, and the footmen began scurrying around with salvers and wine bottles. At a signal from the footman I slipped into the Hall, sat myself at another magnificent instrument situated towards the kitchens, and began playing a string of innocuous pieces by Dibdin, Shield, Salieri, Paisiello – each one fading into the next, the musical equivalent of a trickle of urine. Such meretricious rubbish enabled my mind to be occupied in meditation and observation.

At table a grand (and mostly corpulent) collection of people guzzled their way through an endless series of courses, served from the most magnificent silver and gold dinner service it has ever been this poor man's good fortune to see. I found such gluttony depressing (I have ever been proud of my slim figure). At one stage His Majesty caught my eye and inclined his head most gracefully in my direction. It is not surprising that he is called the First Gentleman of Europe (though not in Europe). For all the apparent fellowship and hearty eating

16

I could not rid myself of a feeling that there was some uneasiness at table. There were short silences, and now and again people looked towards the door. The King himself looked towards the door. But there were no untoward interruptions. As dinner – finally – ended I was led away to a small annex, where I was served a meal in solitary splendour. I ate frugally – merely soup, sturgeon, a loin of veal and a few strawberries with a glass of wine.

At half-past eight the audience was seated in the Music Room, a high, crimson and gold room that was calculated to reduce to insignificance any music except the greatest. I was pleased that I was playing only my own. But even I felt rather small as I walked in, sat down and began my concert. I played two sonatas, and a set of Scottish dances which have proved most popular with lady piano-learners, and which I myself still find it amusing to play now and then. The audience was for the most part attentive, though there were inevitably a few talkers at the back of the room – the sort of people for whom more than half an hour of music is too much. His Majesty was quiet during the playing and generous in leading the applause – he behaved admirably. Indeed, he always does behave well on the level of *manners*, though not always so on the level of *morals*. It was only on one occasion during the concert that the King's concentration faltered and then, once again, he looked nervously towards the door.

When the concert was over, with two trivial but pleasant encore pieces warmly applauded as such pieces always are, I made my bows and retired once more to the North Drawing Room, beside the Music Room. I was immediately approached by a footman with a message from the King: he hoped I would join the Court for the informal supper that would now be taking place. Supper! After that gargantuan guzzling marathon of gluttony! However the invitation was, for an artist, so great an improvement on the practice of the old King's Court (where one sometimes felt one was treated on a level with chimney-sweeps and knife-grinders) that I accepted with pleasure – a pleasure slightly diluted by a fear that I might be forced to fend off a more determined assay on my virtue by the redoubtable Lady Hertford.

17

I had not been ten minutes in the South Drawing Room, receiving the congratulations of the nobility and politicians, when the King made a point of coming over to talk to me.

'Mr Mozart! Another evening of exquisite pleasure to put us still further in your debt. I shake your hand—' he did so, warmly—'I who once tried not to shake but to break it!'

It was beautifully said, and humorously. His manner was singularly sweet and gracious, and though no doubt he condescended, yet there was not a trace of condescension. It was spoken, as far as that was possible, man to man. My heart warmed to him.

'The damage was slight, and we were both young, Your Majesty.'

'That the damage was slight I could *hear* tonight. Such a *style* of execution – none of the younger men have it. Ah, time passes, time passes: you were no more than a boy then, Mr Mozart.'

There seemed to be some sort of implication that more time had passed for me than had for him. Yet seeing us both close up I do not think the impartial observer would have said that this was what our appearances suggested. The King's figure, as the purveyors of caricatures have made so horribly plain, was enormous, like a pig's bladder constricted in a wire cage. And in spite of powder and rouge his face showed very clearly the effects of long years of self-indulgence, both at table and in bed.

'I feel the passing of the years,' I said tactfully.

'Ah, those were palmy days: and so were the days of your wonderful comic operas, before our minds were turned to other, darker things by the French Wars.'

I saw an opening.

'They were indeed happy, prosperous times for me, Your Majesty. I had hoped that with the ending of the wars—'

'—they would return. So did we all. So *do* we all. I was wanting, Mr Mozart, to broach to you a little scheme I have in mind for the Coronation season.'

My heart leapt up, as Mr Wordsworth would say. I bent my head looking profoundly interested, because I was.

'You will agree that English musical life is in need of a

tonic, a stimulus?' he asked. I nodded. How true, I thought: it is in need of a new comic opera by Mozart. 'Now, what I have in mind is a grand gesture – to invite to this country Signor Rossini.'

Rossini! The brass-bandsman's son of Pesaro! The musical chatterer! The charlatan of the crescendo! The brainless, birdlike twitterer! My discomposure could hardly have been more complete. I swallowed.

'He has caught the popular fancy wonderfully, sir.'

'Exactly,' the King said complacently, quite oblivious to my reaction. 'And it would be a great treat for you, wouldn't it? You would learn so much. But we'd want to keep our end up. I'd rely on you, as our senior composer, to show we're not short of native talent.'

Native talent! *Schweinhund!* Is he calling me English? Is he classing me with the Dibdins and the Samuel Wesleys? Does he imagine my name is unknown to the clattering composer from Pesaro?

'Signor Rossini was kind enough to send me the score of his *Barbiere*, with some kind and flattering remarks about my *Figaro*.'

'Is that so? I am impressed. You know, I did wonder whether we could persuade him to run up an opera for the season. What do you think – eh?'

'He does have a quite wonderful . . . facility, sir.'

'Exactly. He'd do it in no time. A fine new opera by Rossini. Perhaps on an English subject. Or Scottish. Something from Sir Walter, perhaps.'

'He has recently . . . *done* his *Lady of the Lake*.'

'*Marmion*, perhaps, then. Something grand and chivalrous. That would be fitting for the ceremonies I plan. Ah, it's all most exciting. Perhaps we could have a concert with the two of you. I shall rely on you, Mr Mozart. I shall make sure that you are kept informed of progress.'

And with a gracious inclination of the head he left me – left me fuming inwardly, and wondering at the charm of his manner and the singular offensiveness of his matter. To class me as an *English* composer, to imply that association with Rossini would be a *treat*, even an *education*! I was fuming so wildly (or as wildly as proper comport-

19

ment at Court would allow) that I neglected to take proper measures of self-protection. There before me was Lady Hertford, all bosom and assertiveness.

'Ah, Mr Mozart!'

'Er . . . My Lady.'

'An evening to remember. Such wonderful musicality and charm. I would like to show my *personal* appreciation—' and to my surprise she produced with great dexterity a purse, handed it to me surreptitiously, and turned her head while I whipped the purse into a pocket with a smoothness born of long practice. 'The King, you understand, has very many calls on his generosity, and is not always able to reward exceptional service as he would wish to do.'

Ah ha! She was saying I was going to get the usual measly twenty guineas, but that she was willing to top it up. Well – all very acceptable.

'I am most grateful to—'

She waved thanks aside with her hand.

'I believe there is talk of an opera season at the Queen's Theatre next year?'

'Preparations are under way, My Lady.'

'Perhaps even a new opera by the great Mozart?'

She smiled, flatteringly and seductively. I was not flattered or seduced.

'That certainly is the intention. With opera companies intention does not always become reality.'

'I believe Lord Hertford is to be involved.'

'I know Mr Popper hopes for his patronage.'

'I have no doubt he will get it. My husband dotes on opera. I believe, in fact, he is to meet Mr Popper next week at the Queen's. Will you be there at the meeting?'

'It is very likely I will be, if plans are to be discussed.'

'Do please keep me informed, Mr Mozart.'

It was said very meaningfully. I was mystified.

'Informed, My Lady?'

'Oh, you know what husbands are like, Mr Mozart!' she said dismissively. 'They never think to tell their wives anything. Remember: I shall rely on you to keep me informed of the arrangements.'

20

And she steamed away, leaving me considerably relieved. She had no designs on my virtue. She had merely been indulging in the amorous small-change of Court life under George IV (where amorous *gestures* are perhaps more frequent than amorous *acts*, remembering the age and figures of most of his courtiers). Her attentions in fact had a quite different motive: she wanted me to spy on her husband, and was willing to pay for my information. I postponed any feeling I might have of being insulted until I had made sure of the extent of her generosity, which I guessed by the weight of the purse to be something in the order of forty guineas or so.

I sipped my glass of wine – a white German wine I could not identify because I was by no means used to wine of such superlative quality. People came up one after another to compliment me on the concert – very kindly, and with as much graciousness as an *English* aristocracy can be expected to muster. I looked for my friend Lord Egremere, whom I had seen at dinner and in the audience at the concert. He was some feet away from me, talking to the King. The King, rumour had it, was wooing the Whigs. Everybody, still, seemed a little on tenterhooks, expecting something . . . I was just wondering what it could be when a footman came up to the King, bowed low, and presented him with a note on a silver plate. The King looked at Lady Hertford, took the note, read it, and swore in a low voice. The two talked for a moment or two, then the King left the Drawing Room in as much discomposure as was compatible with his wonderfully graceful manner.

I looked around me. Everyone seemed to know what news must have been brought to the King. I went over to Lord Egremere. Around us there were signs that supper was forgotten and the assembly was breaking up.

'What has happened, My Lord? Is there bad news?'

'Very bad, though only what everyone has been expecting.'

'Put me out of my suspense. Has Napoleon escaped from St Helena?'

'Worse than that. The Princess has landed at Dover.'

I frowned, uncomprehending.

'The Princess?'

'The Brunswickian. The Queen – only they don't call her that here. The King's wife has landed at Dover.'

The evening was indeed coming to a premature end. I made my way up to my bedroom under a distant tiny cupola smiling with satisfaction.

Nemesis had struck with unusual promptitude. The King had been punished for his boorish insensitivity. That night, for the first time for many years, Prinny and his appalling wife would be sleeping within the same sea-girt isle.

CHAPTER THREE
The Impresario

I was bidden to the meeting at the Queen's Theatre the following Thursday in a little note from Mr Popper asking if I could 'make it convenient' to be there at eleven o'clock, when 'the Lord Hertford' would also be present. Something in the wording of the note suggested that Popper was beginning to suffer not only from the cringe to the rich and powerful which is endemic to those proposing to put on an opera season, but also from the delusions of grandeur which are the concomitant risk. It was something that the presenter of *Janet and Michael* and *Nicholas and Kate* had been only mildly prone to.

When I arrived at the Queen's the Lord Hertford was already comfortably ensconced there in Popper's office, seemingly mightily at home for an aristocrat. The British aristocracy are usually rather good at slumming it in artistic surroundings, which is only fair considering how artists are expected to slum it in pokey ante-rooms when invited to play in their grand mansions. Lord Hertford is an elegant, elderly man with a cool but apparently open manner. The effect that he makes on people is very different to that of his formidable wife but this may be deceptive: it is noticed they are generally united in their aims and ambitions, which are seldom for the general good and usually for the Hertfords' good. He and I are old friends, however, and we exchanged the handshake (I don't know if I mentioned before that I am indebted to him) while he complimented me on my concert before the King at Brighton. When these preliminaries were over I sat down at my ease, though Mr Popper looked as if he thought I should have asked My Lord's permission. He preferred to stride fussily up and down, rubbing his hands.

'Everything is in train,' he said, puffing out his little cheeks, reminding me of some farm bird being fattened for the table. 'Things are shaping up very nicely indeed.'

'You have had replies from Italy?' asked Lord Hertford.

'I have indeed. Both Mme Ardizzi in Naples and Mme Pizzicoli in Venice. So that's capital – a great advance. We shall, if all goes well, have a season of stars. It seems it is only a matter of negotiating their fees.'

'What is the catch?' I asked.

'Eh?'

'What operas do they want specially put on for them?'

'Ah well . . . Mme Ardizzi expresses a wish for *La Vestale*, and Mme Pizzicoli for *Il Re Teodoro* – Paisiello, I believe. And the Viennese lady, as I remember you predicted, Mr Mozart, especially requests *Iphigénie en Tauride*.'

'None of those are operas we could easily mount for just a few performances,' I pointed out.

'Not easily, no.' The cunning look of the impresario came into his eyes. 'Of course they might be found to be impossible to mount when the time came.'

'When the ladies are here and the season well under way,' I agreed. 'Similar discoveries have been made in the past. It has been made clear to the ladies, has it, that they are to have parts in my *Le Donne Allegre*?'

'Oh yes.' There came over him a shuffling air, equally characteristic of the opera impresario. 'Mme Hubermann-Cortino expressed herself delighted at the prospect of singing in a new piece by such a consummate musician.'

'And the other ladies?'

'Ah . . . Mme Ardizzi said nothing on the subject . . . Er, Mme Pizzicoli – I'm sorry to have to say it, my dear sir – said she wondered that we should be performing a work by such a stale composer as you – I use her own words, of course.'

I immedialtely conceived a feeling of warmth for Mme

24

Hubermann-Cortino, clearly a singer of great discernment, and a German to boot, and an aversion to the Italian ladies, whose voices were doubtless as empty as their heads. Bird song and bird brains almost invariably go together in operatic prima donnas. My Lord Hertford hurried in with soothing words.

'No one who heard your last symphony for the Philharmonic Society could conceivably find you dated, my dear Mozart. The lady clearly hasn't heard your recent works.'

'I think she has heard *La Clemenza di Tito*,' said Mr Popper sourly. Talk of my last opera, written for the victorious sovereigns after Waterloo, whom it bored prodigiously, always puts me in a tetchy humour which Mr Popper, who lost a deal of money on the opera, knows very well. I was clearly only at the meeting to be shown my place. His next remark was not calculated to mollify me.

'I have heard rumours of a visit by Rossini.'

'A whim of the King's,' said Lord Hertford dismissively.

'I have heard rumours of a commission for an opera from him.'

'A pipe-dream,' said My Lord in the same manner. 'The man is notoriously lazy.'

'But capable of great bursts of activity,' returned Popper. 'There are still nine months before the Coronation, My Lord.'

'You should not believe the stories of operas being dashed off in three days,' I said with some irritation. 'Operas *cannot* be dashed off in three days. It is physically impossible. The man has a genius for publicity.'

'Besides,' said Lord Hertford expansively, 'who would put it on? Covent Garden?'

We all sniggered.

'Hardly,' I said. 'The place hasn't been a serious musical theatre for years. And since they increased the prices no one can afford to go.'

'Where else would it be performed but here at the Queen's?' asked Mr Popper. I knew immediately what *that* would mean for the production of my new opera. Before I could speak Lord Hertford hurried in with emollient words.

'It would hardly be possible to produce new works by Mr Mozart and Signor Rossini in one short season,' he said. 'And we are undoubtedly honoured by the prospect of mounting Mr Mozart's piece at the Queen's. By the by, Popper, you should give some thought to changing the name of this place. When we put on Mozart's piece we'll certainly be hoping for the attendance of the King. And you can hardly expect him to come to a theatre called the Queen's.'

He had succeeded in changing the subject. Mr Popper was interested.

'It was named after his respected mother,' he said pompously. 'But I confess the thought had occurred to me. I was outside Alderman Wood's yesterday morning. . .'

I should explain, should this account come to be read by future generations, that Queen Caroline had made a triumphant progress from Dover to London and was now lodged at the home of one of her most vociferous supporters, a man called Alderman Wood. This last was a loud-mouthed trouble-maker, and the Queen's move was as unwise a one as could be expected even of her. However the mob streamed to the place to roar their support, and the Queen's many appearances before them to acknowledge support increased their enthusiasm beyond all bounds.

'Ah,' said Lord Hertford, leaning forward much intrigued. 'And how was Her Majesty – Her Royal Highness, I should say – looking? It is many years since I had the . . . interesting experience of seeing her.'

'I tell you, Mr Lord,' said Mr Popper with feeling, 'the counter of a Manchester tallow-chandler's would not be graced by her presence behind it. She is fat, rouged, deplorably dressed and her manners are of the most vulgar and familiar. It is difficult to believe that she was a Princess.'

'German,' said Lord Hertford. 'The princelings of that country combine petty tyranny with democratic manners and plebeian standards of cleanliness.' I fumed! Are not Austria and Germany one? Are they not My Country?

26

Lord Hertford, more sensitive than his lordly manner might lead one to expect, actually noticed. 'Oh, sorry, Mozart. Forgot you were a bit of a Hun yourself. But the Princess does no credit to your nation. For my part I always took care not to stand to windward of her.'

'Certainly the King will not want to be reminded of her by the name of this theatre,' I said, to avoid further aggravation. Hun! 'What could it be changed to?'

Mr Popper held up his hand.

'I said the thought occurred to me. I did not say I had decided on it. You did not see the mob at Alderman Wood's, My Lord. They would not take kindly to anything that smacked of an insult to her. Mark my words, we're in for a period of mob rule, and while the fuss lasts I'm not going to consider changing our name.'

For once something Mr Popper said made sense. Lord Hertford nodded gravely.

'A very good point, and a sobering thought. As a matter of fact they've been to my house already. Threw a lot of stones, but no great harm done. Now, about that other business, Popper – the girl I brought along with me.'

I pricked up my ears.

'Ah yes, of course . . .' Mr Popper lost his brief authority of manner. He was obviously anticipating that Lord Hertford was expecting a quid pro quo for his promised financial support. 'Well, I'm very happy to hear her, My Lord . . . I can make no promises, of course.'

'Nor would I believe any you made. There are many considerations other than musical talent that you have to take into account when you are casting your pieces, that I know. But there are small parts, and she might be kept in reserve, in case of sickness. . .'

'By all means. Let's have her in.'

Lord Hertford got up, so I did.

'I thought you should hear her in the theatre, Popper. She is essentially a creature of the theatre. If we could go through to the Circle. . .'

'Very well, My Lord. You will accompany her, Mr Mozart?'

'No need, no need,' said Lord Hertford, waving his

hand. 'She has her own accompanist with her. I am particularly anxious that Mr Mozart should hear her in the best possible circumstances.'

So we trooped through to the foyer, where a young lady and gentleman were waiting. I was flattered by Lord Hertford's special consideration for me, but I was also anxious to get a good look at the young lady from close to. However a poke bonnet and a demure demeanour prevented me. The young gentleman was a handsome, well-set-up sprig. Lord Hertford directed the pair through the stalls and towards the stage.

When we got to the Circle and took our seats in the front row the young man was sitting down at the fortepiano which was in the pit. He set up his music and improvised a few flourishes at the keyboard.

'Ee – tha's got a raight tinny instrument thee-ar!'

The young lady emerged from the wings. Gone were the poke bonnet, and gone too any trace of the demure demeanour. She had a striking figure, excellent carriage and she walked on to the stage as if she was born on it – taking command of it and filling it. If I call her beautiful that will perhaps convey the wrong impression, but she had fine raven tresses and strong features that would tell well on stage. And she was right about the fortepiano.

'Ee, well: needs must when t'devil drives. Médée's aria from Act III of *Médée*. Cherubini.'

The cheekiness with which she added the composer's name was wonderful. For here was an oddity: she was to sing part of an opera that had never been heard in London. It was much admired in France – I much admired it myself, within reason. Yet, unless she had travelled on the Continent the young lady could only know it by the score. A musical and sophisticated young lady, then, whose Yorkshire accent was some kind of joke on us. When I looked back at the stage she was crouched there in an attitude of rage, desperation and despair, and as her pianist tried to coax the requisite passion out of his poor instrument she began sculpting the phrases of Monsieur Cherubini to express the torn nature of that terrible creature, swaying between mother-love and a desire for

28

the most frightful revenge of all.

'What did she say the piece was?' asked Mr Popper.

'Cherubini's *Médée*. A fine opera.'

'And her name?' he asked, turning to Lord Hertford.

'Betty Ackroyd.'

She sang as finely as she acted, in a clear, full soprano that seemed equal to any dramatic or musical demands she made on it. When the piece finished the singer rose to her feet, went upstage, and stood with her back to us. I heard from the pianist the opening bars from Act II of my *Figaro*. It was many years since I had heard them, and I confess I was moved. The singer turned, and, moving downstage with consummate grace and aristocratic deportment, she launched into the opening phrases of 'Porgi Amor' with such control, such dignity and style, that I had to wipe away a tear. Yes, she chose the piece because she knew I would be listening to her. But oh! she knew how to sing it to tear at the heartstrings.

'Pretty piece,' said Popper. 'What is it?'

When my heartbreaking lament for a love that has faded was over, she came centre-stage and winked at us.

'Here's something for t'gallery.'

And the pianist threw himself into – again he came up! – Rossini. But not just any jangly piece familiar from the barrel organs, but the finale of *La Donna del Lago* – new music, unknown here, not known to me except in the score, and done by the singer with such affecting grace, both of voice and of personality, that even my heart leapt.

When she finished the piece she curtsied to us, the pianist bowed, and they both left the stage.

'What's your opinion?' asked Popper, turning to me. His musical ignorance is legendary. He could have heard the great Farinelli and not been sure what to think of him. I knew I had to speak in superlatives to get through to him.

'Exceptional. Quite exceptional. A brilliant voice, excellent musicianship, and a wonderful stage presence and ability to convey the drama of a piece.'

'Ah, you like her. You think we could use her?'

'I do indeed.'

'What in, do you think? *Susan and Frederick*?'

29

'NOT *Susan and Frederick*. And not *The Wizard of Wolverhampton*. All you need for them is pretty voices. This is not a pretty voice: it is a great voice, a voice for connoisseurs.'

'I agree with Mr Mozart,' put in Lord Hertford. 'It is not a voice for burlesques. She is trained for opera, temperamentally suited only to *great* music – or at least *dramatic* music. She is singing in *The Creation* in September.'

'Then we must find her something,' said Mr Popper, mindful of who his paymaster was. 'Leave it to me and Mr Mozart. We shall find her something suitable. Do you, My Lord, find her an Italian name before she sings in the Haydn.'

He knew who composed *The Creation*. Marvel of marvels!

'Why not emphasise her Englishness?' I suggested. 'The prima donna from – where is she from, My Lord?'

'From Bradford.'

But even as I said it, it didn't sound quite right. Mr Popper groaned, and waved the suggestion aside.

'It's been tried before, and it never works. The English expect their opera singers to be Italian – continental, anyway. No, no, call her Mme Montezuma or something.'

'Montezuma was a native Mexican emperor,' I put in acidly. 'It would suggest, musically, nothing so much as primitive chants.'

'Well, anyway, something of the sort. And now, Mr Mozart, Lord Hertford and I have financial matters to talk over. . .'

He looked at me as if I knew nothing about money – I who have made an art form out of managing slender resources! I took the hint and withdrew. The financing of an opera season is something I have no desire to be involved in. My personal finances take up quite enough of my time. As I trod the steps down to the foyer I saw that the young couple were there, and apparently waiting for someone. As I gained the bottom Betty Ackroyd came over to me, sank into a curtsey, and said: 'Allow me to salute the greatest musician of our age!'

30

Now that was gratifying! She had discarded the Northern speech which I had already decided was a tease or an affectation and spoke with simple admiration. The young man too came over and shook my hand.

'Bradley Hartshead. I am honoured to meet you, Mr Mozart.'

'It is equally a pleasure to meet two such fine musicians,' I said with truth. 'There are not too many people who can coax expressiveness from that "tinny instrument".' I turned to Betty Ackroyd. 'And you, Ma'am: such fire and intelligence from one so young! I have seldom in my life heard so promising a singer. And not just a singer: you took to the stage of the Queen's as if you had been on it all your life.'

'We came on Monday,' said Bradley Hartshead, 'to hear you directing the performance of *Janet and Michael*.'

'How does it come about,' asked Betty Ackroyd, without the intention of giving offence, 'that the greatest composer of our age is forced to grub for a living directing offal?'

A good question! Because my revered father was dazzled and beguiled by a purse of fifty guineas from the sovereign of these benighted islands. But I could not say that.

'Ah well, as it happens that was offal I composed,' I said.

'Put together, perhaps. Dashed off while your mind was mainly occupied with the pleasures of a game pie or a glass of good claret. The music you have *composed* differs from that as fine linen differs from shoddy.'

She had gone to the heart of the matter at once.

'Well well, you may be right,' I said.

'If I should be so happy as to sing one of the roles in an opera by you, I should consider it the greatest honour in my life!'

'Then let us hope that you do, and let us hope that I direct you. In fact, I anticipate with great pleasure working with you – you both – in the future.'

I bowed. He bowed. She curtsied, and they left the theatre, walking in the direction of the park. Clearly they had been waiting for me. I turned down towards St James's, feeling warm and flattered, but my mind ticking away the while.

Bradford. I know a little about these Northern towns,

through my son Charles Thomas who teaches in Wakefield, having married a lady of that town. Bradford is not very far from Wakefield. It is also not very far from Leeds. And Leeds is the city close to which Lord Hertford, through Lady Hertford, has one of his several grand houses.

Clearly he had found something to interest him up there.

It was with reluctance that evening that I wrote to Lady Hertford. I have no relish for the role of spy. The business of My Lord Hertford is his own business, and I would have thought that his wife would, in view of her own relationship with His Majesty, allow him a certain latitude. However rationality flies out the window when love is involved, or that is my experience: *così fan tutte* – or rather *tutti*. Unfortunately in the present case I had no choice. The purse which Her Ladyship had slipped to me at Brighton had indeed contained no less than forty guineas – making, with the King's measly reward, a satisfying sixty guineas. I could not, of course, compromise my honour. But neither could I accept the money and not send her some kind of a report. And the money had certainly been accepted, because somehow it had been spent. After prolonged consideration I penned the following note.

To The Most Hon. The Marchioness of Hertford.
Madam,

At Your Ladyship's request I hereby send you a report of the progress of the proposed Italian Opera Season at the Queen's Theatre. At the meeting on Thursday Mr Popper informed us that the negotiations with the *prime donne* who will undoubtedly form the backbone of the proposed company are well under way, and Mmes Ardizzi, Pizzicoli and Hubermann-Cortino have all expressed their great interest. Mr Popper and My Lord Hertford also had discussions about the financial aspects of the season, though that was a discussion I did not feel inclined – or qualified – to attend.

Lord Hertford introduced us to the talents of Miss

32

Elizabeth Ackroyd, from Bradford. These seemed to me to be very considerable, and I have no doubt she will be an asset to the company in the proposed season.

Your Ladyship's generous acknowledgment of my concert at Brighton is greatly appreciated. I have the honour to remain Your Ladyship's obedient servant
                    Wolfgang Gottlieb Mozart.

I sent the letter on its way, uncertain whether I had given the lady what she wanted but hoping that she would expect no more from me for her forty guineas. Knowing the fashionable world as I do I had the sinking feeling that she would in fact expect a great deal more.

CHAPTER FOUR
The Queen of the Night

The months that followed were among the most curious of my life, for never before (apart, perhaps, from the time of the Gordon riots, when I felt particularly threatened on account of my religion) had I had the sense that I and the rest of polite London were in the hands of the mob. A Frenchman told me that it reminded him of Paris in 1789. Please do not misunderstand me: I have nothing (well, little) but admiration for Englishmen of the lower order. As a Mason I believe that enlightenment must with time spread to all classes, and that with education and an enlargement of his understanding the English worker will be as sober of judgment as an Englishman of the better class or a workman in my beloved Germany.

But yet a mob in the grip of a wrong-headed notion is a fearsome thing. And on the surface their sympathy for the Queen seemed both just and generous. For the King to propose to put her, in effect, on trial before the House of Lords for licentious conduct was to invite scrutiny of his own morals, about which the whole nation knew all too much. The mob had no doubts that, at best, he was as guilty as his spouse, and they greeted him on his infrequent public appearances with boos and catcalls, so that he retreated to Royal Lodge, Windsor, thus adding cowardice to the legion of charges against him. Yet for all its generosity, the verdict of the mob was decidedly wrong-headed: the stories in the highest circles about her behaviour, and the behaviour she tried to encourage *in her own daughter*, proved that the current darling of the streets was a woman of the most tawdry and shop-soiled variety.

All this is a matter of public record. On a personal level the consequences of 'Queen fever' were perhaps no worse than being forced to cheer the Queen, toast the Queen, give public testimony to the virtue of the Queen. My Lord Hertford was worst affected, being the husband of the King's mistress, and his town house was frequently the target of the mob's wrath and contempt.

'I blame the King,' said Mr Popper.

It is of course usual for the common people (and people, in my experience, are rarely more common than opera impresarios) to blame their rulers for every ill under the sun, including bad weather. But Mr Popper did have a point.

'If the silly man had simply ignored his wife none of this would have happened,' he went on.

It was quite true that if the King had not been determined to divorce his Caroline, cut her out of the Prayer book, prevent her attendance at his lavish (i.e. totally ostentatious and unspiritual) Coronation ceremony, the opera season would not have been threatened as it was.

Let me explain. The Queen had spent much of her time since her separation from the King in Italy, where she had collected around her an entourage of dubious and insalubrious characters, among them her lover Pergami. When in due time the House of Lords came to consider evidence for her licentious conduct, most of the witnesses against her were inevitably Italians, testifying in their own language or a most curious version of English (often learned from the Queen herself, who had never mastered it). The mob drew their own irrational conclusions, and all Italians became potential victims of their wrath. Innocent ice-cream sellers were stoned and organ-grinders and their monkeys pelted with rotten vegetables. Potential witnesses were met at Dover with terrifying evidences of the mob's hatred. Quite soon the Crown's supply of witnesses simply dried up. They refused to come and testify, no matter what the financial inducement was.

News of the anti-Italian feeling got quickly back to Italy. Prime donne are not the bravest of individuals. Vain, blatant, greedy, promiscuous, vulgar – in my experience they can be any (or, frequently, all) of those things, but brave, very seldom. First Mme Pizzicoli wrote to Mr Popper saying she had heard of the unspeakable outrages inflicted on her fellow countrymen by the disgraceful English mob, and in sympathy for the sufferings of those poor innocents she would deny the English the joy of hearing her voice. 'No great loss,' I said, remembering her previous letter. 'I believe she has no taste at all.' A week later came a letter in similar vein from Mme Ardizzi. The Coronation season was left with the prospect of Mme Hubermann-Cortino as its sole prima donna. Mr Popper decided she would be known as Mme Hubermann. 'Simpler,' he said. He clearly expected the anti-Italian feeling to last.

In the meantime my acquaintance with Betty Ackroyd and Bradley Hartshead was ripening. Some days after our first meeting she wrote me a sweet little note saying that she was singing my *Exsultate Jubilate* with an amateur band in Clerkenwell, and wondered whether she could sing it for me first and get my advice. Thus began an association that brought me nothing but pleasure. During those hot summer months of the Queen's 'trial' Betty or Bradley Hartshead or both together would come to my rooms to play and sing my music to me and discuss finer points of interpretation or wider questions of music theory. I coached Betty in the soprano part of *The Creation*, which brought poignantly back to me the London visits of my dear old friend Haydn. When she sang the role of Eve, with great success, it was as Elizabeth Ackroyd: Mr Popper would in other circumstances have preferred her to adopt a foreign name nobody could pronounce for the opera season, but now an assumed Italian name was out of the question, and as to a German one – who could know what was about to be alleged about the Queen's girlhood years in Brunswick?

It was Betty who brought me the good news about Rossini.

'We hear that Rossini is not coming,' she said, taking off her cloak as she entered my apartment.

'Really?'

'Declines His Majesty's most gracious invitation.'

'How did you hear?'

'Lord Hertford told me.'

'So cowardice and concern for creature comforts have triumphed,' I said. 'I knew they would. What reason did he give?'

'Pressure of work. He is engaged on *Matilde di Shabran* for a theatre in Rome.'

'Another deathless opus from the hand of the master,' I said, chuckling. 'And one who is supposed to rattle them off in five or six days! All the better! More chance for my *Donne Gaie di Windsor*. With you as Alice Ford – or perhaps Anne Page. Now Popper won't be able to get out of it.'

The opera was really going very well, musically speaking. I was already beginning the last scene of all, in the forest. I had banged the head of my doltish (no, extremely cultivated – that was the problem) librettist, and in the end something reasonably shapely and dramatic had been cobbled together by the two of us. I had, fortunately, rare peace in which to compose. Beyond occasional appearances at the fortepiano to direct performances of *The Baker's Daughter of Westminster* or whatever piece of nonsense I had let trickle from my pen in a fit of absence of mind, I had little to do. I left to Mr Popper the ordeals of putting together an opera company. He could put up with the tantrums of tenors who never can acknowledge their essential secondariness in an opera company; he could put up with the fumings of husbands of sopranos, who disguise their cuckoldry with furious bluster. All I gathered was that due to the cravenness of the Italian singers Betty Ackroyd and other singers from Northern Europe were to play a bigger part in the season than had been anticipated. This pleased me. I found too that Mr Popper had decided to prepare Betty by giving her parts in the burlesques with which he enriched the cultural life of the capital. This pleased me less. You do not learn how to sing my Countess or Herr Gluck's Iphigenia by appearing as the baker's daughter of Wherever. However Betty Ackroyd seemed already to

37

know how to sing my Countess and Iphigenia, so I rejoiced that she had a regular income, and welcomed the fact that I occasionally saw her at the theatre, in addition to our sessions when we went through my own music and that of other truly great composers, including that of Handel, without which no festivities of the beef-witted English would be complete.

Both Betty and Bradley Hartshead were at the Queen's Theatre on the fateful day. We had in fact been rehearsing a curtain-raiser I had dashed off one day while seated, constipated, on the stool of ease, and we were in the foyer about to issue forth through the main entrance into the Haymarket when a carriage drew up outside. It was a perfectly ordinary, anonymous carriage, so imagine my astonishment when from it stepped, hurriedly and furtively, My Lord Hertford, turning to hand down – something – a woman – a girl, such as I would not have expected to see him publicly associate with. Her face was shaded, but she was dressed in a threadbare grey worsted cloak, with a hood, underneath which one could see a dress that was none of the cleanest, holed hose, and shoes that were cracked. Lord Hertford bundled her through the doors, across the foyer, nodding to us in a preoccupied manner, and straight down the corridor that led to Mr Popper's office, which he walked into without knocking and shut the door behind him and the mysterious creature.

We immediately decided that we were not after all in any haste to leave the theatre.

Our persistence there was rewarded. It was some ten minutes later, when we were still discussing who the woman could possibly be, that Mr Popper issued from his office and approached our little group down the corridor.

'Ah – ahem – Mr Mozart – glad you are still here. I wonder if you could favour us with a few minutes of your valuable time. And Miss Ackroyd too. It is a matter of some delicacy, Mr Hartshead, so perhaps. . .'

He was quite unusually polite. That should have worried me, and I should have manufactured some excuse and left – as Bradley Hartshead immediately did with the tact and delicacy with which he did everything. But the prospect of perhaps doing a favour for Lord Hertford, to whom I am indebted, persuaded me otherwise, as doubtless it did Betty Ackroyd. We allowed ourselves to be led along the corridor into Popper's office.

Lord Hertford was sitting in a chair, once more his usual easy yet commanding self. But our eyes were drawn to the other figure. Huddled on the sofa, the cloak now open and revealing the full extent of her grubby clothing, was a scrap of a girl – not short, but thin, weaselly of feature, and pathetic. Her face, already dirty, had come to resemble a relief map through the runnels of tears. She was snivelling now, then looking up at us beseechingly as if craving protection.

'This is Jenny,' said Lord Hertford.

There was silence. Eventually I looked at him enquiringly.

'And Jenny is—?'

'A most important person,' said Lord Hertford, smiling at her and trying to reach her on her own level. 'Someone whose presence here needs to be concealed from the mob.' A sob came from the bundle on the sofa. Lord Hertford cleared his throat, conscious he had made a false step. 'There is therefore no question of her being installed, however secretly, in any of my houses, or my wife's. Each has a large staff whose loyalty, though considerable, cannot be guaranteed or absolute. There is always one who, for money or out of misplaced enthusiasm, will betray their master. Do I make myself understood?'

'Oh, absolutely,' said Mr Popper.

'So I bethought me of the theatre, where she might both live – her wants are modest – and serve her turn usefully, perhaps as a dresser, until she is required. She need never, in fact, go out into the streets, and rarely be seen outside a single dressing-room. Now I thought that Miss Ackroyd, for example, who is starting on the lower rungs of the theatrical ladder, has not yet got a dresser of her own. . .'

'No . . .' said Betty Ackroyd doubtfully, as if this scrap of humanity was hardly what she would freely have chosen, left to herself. A dresser is a protector and defender, a safe

39

haven from storms. This pathetic specimen of humanity looked as far from a protector as it was possible to get. But of course if Lord Hertford suggested it . . . She nodded her agreement.

'You say until she is required —' I interjected.

'Ah yes. That is a matter which we must keep entirely between ourselves. She is – but perhaps she can tell you herself.' He looked a mite dubious though, as he gazed at his charge. 'Tell the lady and gentleman who you are, Jenny.'

After a long pause a tiny squeak emerged from the meagre bundle of rags on the sofa.

'Jenny.'

'Yes – Jenny what?'

'Jenny Bowles.'

'And tell them where you've worked up to now.'

That seemed quite beyond her, but after a long wait there came tiny sounds that I interpreted as 'Mr Woods'. Lord Hertford looked at us, but only saw us looking bewilderedly at each other.

'At Alderman Woods,' he said significantly.

Now our looks were charged with dawning comprehension. Alderman Woods – where the Queen had stayed when she first arrived back in London, before she moved to more suitable accommodation in Brandenburg House, in Hammersmith. Lord Hertford turned back to Jenny Bowles.

'Now tell the lady and gentleman – no, wait: I'll tell them myself, and you nod if I'm getting it right.' She nodded feebly, and he looked at her intently as he resumed. 'Jenny is a scullery maid at Alderman Wood's house in South Audley Street. She is sweet on one of the gardening boys there.' (Impossible to imagine!) 'One night, while the Queen was staying as Alderman Wood's guest Jenny went out of the house late at night to meet her sweetheart in the garden.' Jenny hung her head, gazing fixedly at her lap. Lord Hertford became avuncular. 'No need to be ashamed of that, Jenny! Perfectly natural. Look at me, Jenny, to see that I get this right. When you and your sweetheart parted you were at the front of the house, in fact in an alleyway

40

opposite. You were about to make your way along the street and round to the back of the house, to let yourself back through the kitchen entrance, which you had a key to, when you heard voices approaching the house along the street. Right? You stayed there in the alley, because you recognised the voice of your master and you didn't wish to be seen by him. Will you nod if that's right? . . . Good. He came up to the door with two men. Will you tell the people what sort of men they were, Jenny?'

The scrap said squeakily: 'Big.'

Lord Hertford suppressed a sigh.

'Yes, that's right: big men. You learned from the talk what they were, didn't you?'

There was a long, long pause for thought, then one word came:

'Watermen.'

The watermen man the ferries and harbours of London, conveying passengers, humping cargo. They are big, tough men whose work is hard, unremitting, insalubrious toil. They are also men who seem to regard washing as detracting from their manhood. They omit, consequently, an extremely strong odour of masculinity.

'But what on earth could—?' I began. I was pulled up by a suppressed burst of laughter from Betty Ackroyd behind me. 'You can't mean that—?'

'It is, I agree, all but incredible,' said Lord Hertford, managing to keep a straight face. 'Even of the Queen I could hardly have imagined it possible. Unfortunately the conversation of Alderman Wood with the two men renders the matter quite incontrovertible: it was all too painfully clear.'

I have to say that My Lord did not actually convey any sense that he found the idea painful. In fact I had the feeling that, underneath his frigid exterior, there was a sense of triumph.

'The watermen have always been great supporters of the Queen,' I said thoughtfully.

'They would be, wouldn't they?'

'They have cheered her wherever she has gone. I did not detect any irony in the cheers.'

41

'They are hardly masters of irony. I have no doubt the story has got around them. It may well be that those two were not the only ones. Even if they were, the stories they could tell. . .'

'Of course we would not want to hear details,' I began tentatively.

Lord Hertford nodded.

'Suffice it to say that a three-to-a-bed arrangement was mooted, with some detail which I could not go into with ladies present as to what . . . er . . . should subsequently take place in that bed.'

'But the young lady, Jenny, has been able to report the exact words spoken on this occasion?' I probed.

'She has. Without, of course, precisely understanding their significance.'

This time Betty Ackroyd managed to keep a straight face. Lord Hertford paused for a few minutes, deep in thought.

'It is now the first week in October. We have a brief pause before the Queen's supporters present their case to the Lords,' he said pensively.

'That is a point,' said Mr Popper, who I rather thought did not like his present situation. 'The "Case for the Prosecution", if we may call it that, is complete.'

'It can be reopened,' said Lord Hertford, with a wave of his hand. 'That was allowed for when the case was closed, so many of the witnesses having been intimidated. So we have an unexpected, last-minute witness, and one whose testimony will be all the more telling since the matter concerns the Queen's conduct not in Italy but *in this realm*; and not in the past, but *now* . . . The defence witnesses start to give evidence next week. Rumour has it they will be unimpeachable. Rumour has it they are a gang of scoundrels. Rumour has whatever you want to hear and whatever you don't want to hear. We must wait and see. No one can be more conscious than I that the prosecution witnesses were not impressive. I have a hunch that the defence ones will be still less so. They will have to be questioned remorselessly. I would think it will be a month at the very least, and more probably two, before we can produce our trump card.'

As he talked my mind – and no doubt Betty Ackroyd's

mind, and perhaps even Mr Popper's feeble apology for a mind – had been bubbling over with questions: how had this girl and her story come to Lord Hertford's attention? Was her story true? How could she be given the confidence to testify before the Lords? At his last words our eyes inevitably, but unfortunately, strayed to the figure on the sofa. It was impossible to imagine a human being who looked less like a trump card.

CHAPTER FIVE
Mlle Silberklang

In the days that succeeded the advent of Jenny I found myself going more and more often to the Queen's Theatre. Not, you understand, to see that particular fragment of humanity, but to register how the secret of her identity was being kept, and to wonder what was the likely effect of her testifying before the enquiry into the Queen's conduct at the House of Lords.

It was impossible to imagine her testifying. Absolutely impossible. Even in a court of law, with a kindly and encouraging judge – not, in my experience of insolvency proceedings, a common phenomenon – one could not imagine her giving comprehensible evidence. Even before three or four of us Lord Hertford had had to lead her through her experience – or rather take the major part of the telling on himself. Imagine her in that Chamber, facing the full panoply of state, the country's nobles in serried ranks, their bejewelled and overdressed wives in the galleries – no: it was simply impossible.

Of course I wondered how Betty was getting on with her. If I called in on her in her newly-acquired dressing-room there would be Jenny in a corner, ironing or darning in what looked like an inexpert manner. One day Betty got rid of her by sending her to borrow a scarf from a fellow singer.

'How is she progressing?' I asked, in a conspiratorial whisper.

Betty shrugged.

'She does what I tell her if I show her how.'

'Does she get any better?'

'Well, yes, I suppose so, though she's far from bright and not a needlewoman. That's not the problem.'

'What is?'

'She will never in a million years be a *dresser*,' said Betty, as if she'd been twenty years in the theatre. 'A dresser is a personality, a force. Can you imagine Jenny being a force?'

Exactly what I had expected.

'No I can't,' I said. 'Do you and she talk?'

'Oh yes. Or rather I talk a lot to her. She answers a little. But talking to me is not like giving evidence to the House of Lords, is it?'

I agreed it was not. Betty began talking to Jenny while I was there in the dressing-room, but she seldom got more than monosyllabic squeaks in reply. What could the Lord Chancellor do with monosyllabic squeaks? I noticed that Betty watched and listened to Jenny most intently, and I formed the notion that she was thinking of using her as the basis for a comic performance – I could not think in what: no piece that I know of has a character of such embarrassing inarticulateness.

The theatre was jumpy. This should not have been so, since the secret was known to only three people who were regularly there: Betty, Mr Popper and myself. What must have been happening was that nervousness was being communicated outwards, like ripples from a stone thrown into a pond. It was not difficult to guess which of the three was giving rise to the ripples.

One day, five or six days after Jenny's arrival, and before the hearings on the Queen's adultery – and hence her treason – were resumed, I was talking about repertoire with Edward Clarkson, who directs performances most of the evenings when I am not there myself. Repertoire is not really my business: I compose, and I direct from time to time the pap I and others have composed. But he respects my judgment, and indeed calls on the vast knowledge I have built up over the years of the endless feeble burlesques English composers have thrown together to fill the two hours' traffic of the English musical stage.

'We will need three new pieces to fill the time before the

opera season,' Clarkson was saying. 'Or rather *old* pieces, because nothing I have been shown recently could conceivably be thrown on stage.'

I considered.

'If the audiences can't have novelty, perhaps they could have a piece they have forgotten, or are too young to have known. One of the older Dibdin pieces, for example.'

'It's a thought,' agreed Clarkson. He meditated for a moment. 'One of the early ones with the dialogue freshened up, perhaps. What about *The Waterman?*'

'WHAT?'

It was Mr Popper, who had been passing. He had sprung round all red, as if a bee had got into his britches and stung his bottom. I jumped, so to speak, into the breach.

'The old Dibdin piece,' I said, with affected casualness. 'Before your time, I expect: *The Waterman* – quite a jolly affair, and with one or two pleasant tunes.'

He spluttered for a few more moments.

'I know *The Waterman* perfectly well. An impossibly feeble piece. We will *not* do *The Waterman.*'

And he went on with such dignity as he could muster.

Mr Clarkson raised his eyebrows.

'I've always thought it one of Dibdin's stronger works,' he said, but made no further comment.

Was rumour getting around? That was what worried me. Why did I worry? Simple self-interest. If the Queen's reputation was destroyed by Jenny Bowles, and if the Queen's Theatre played its part in concealing and protecting her, then the opera season, and my delightful contribution to it, were assured of royal patronage. Prinny would steam in to opera after opera, dispensing his own brand of graciousness, buoyed up – if it is possible to imagine so heavy a human load buoyed up – by the public approbation of the fickle mob.

But if the rumour got out . . .?

I was accosted one evening in the vestibule of the Queen's Theatre before a performance of my – something or other – one of my dribbled pieces – by Lord Harewood.

'Hear you're putting something together for the opera season, Mr Mozart.'

I do not regard myself as indebted to Lord Harewood. What is more, he has no ear for music at all. He is dedicated to Acquisition, and music cannot be acquired.

'I am *composing* an opera, My Lord,' I said coldly.

'That's the ticket. Time we had another by you. Something along the lines of *Il Matrimonio Segreto*, eh? That was a capital piece – one of your best.' His elephantine attempts at ingratiation over, he pointed to the other side of the crowded vestibule. 'Something going on over there, eh?'

He was pointing, in fact, towards the door into the auditorium, where Mr Popper was deep in murmured conversation with Lord Hertford. Mr Popper had assumed his air of turkey-cock self importance – a ludicrous stance to those who knew his indecisive character and general incompetence – while Lord Hertford, though never losing his air of somewhat distant affability, nevertheless had an undoubtedly conspiratorial air. I saw Betty Ackroyd, who was not performing that evening, watching them both and setting her body into the ridiculous strutting posture of Mr Popper. I knew by now that the basis of her acting skills was in observation and mimicry.

'Undoubtedly something is up,' I said, still very chilly. 'Lord Hertford is the principal patron for the Coronation opera season you alluded to.'

'Ah!' said Lord Harewood, with a funny sort of smile. 'Think that's it, do you?'

'Of course. An opera season demands a great deal of planning.'

'And a great deal of money. Hmmm. Perhaps you're right. But in my experience of recent weeks, when people are talking *like that* they're always talking about the Queen.'

He was right, of course. Lord Harewood, though unmusical, was far from a fool. But was he right from a general worldly wisdom, or because rumours had reached his noble ears? And if they had, I doubted whether Mr Popper – from sheer fear – would be the one who had talked. That left Betty Ackroyd. But I discarded that thought immediately. I *knew* Betty: if she was sworn to

47

silence she would *be* silent. It must be Popper's damned jumpiness giving rise to rumours.

The day that the Queen's defence began at the Palace of Westminster was in any case – I mean even without the event I am about to narrate – a day of tension and excitement. It became clear subsequently as the days of evidence proceeded, that the witnesses for the Queen's probity and purity were every bit as unimpressive as the witnesses for her flagrant immorality had been – perhaps more so, for they were on occasion so awed by the majesty of their surroundings that they actually spoke the truth. 'It is fortunate that the place never affects the Lords themselves like that,' said Lord Hertford wittily. 'Otherwise party government would become impossible.' But on that first day of the defence no one knew the names or the quality of the witnesses, so everyone was more jumpy than ever.

It was late in the afternoon, as the theatre was buzzing with rumours brought back from Westminster by Lord Hertford and others, when a particularly fine carriage drew up outside the Queen's Theatre. It was, I learned later, one of the carriages of the Fitzroy Hotel, and it had been put at the disposal of one of the hotel's guests completely free of charge by an enraptured hotel manager. Why are such gestures only made to beautiful women? If they were made to elderly, infirm gentlemen I should be relieved of the necessity of defaulting on payment. But to return to our muttons. The smart coachman leapt down and whipped quickly round to pull down the step and open the carriage door, standing so stiffly to attention that one might imagine the figure to emerge would be one of the royal dukes. But no such ill luck.

She was beautiful in the manner of all beautiful German women – that is, more beautiful than any other nation's beautiful women. She was fair, her hair luxuriant and immaculately coiffed; her skin was fair too, a creamy white, and her features were regular and charming. Her figure was in every way imposing – fuller than the English like, but in every way enticing. How did I know she was foreign, that she was German? I do not know, but I did. Perhaps it was like speaking through the air-waves to like. Perhaps it was just because she was not *ordinary*.

'What has such a creature to do with Mr Popper?' I said to Andrew Masters, the tenor, who was standing beside me.

'Or with any mortal male?' he breathed, and though he is stupid in the manner of all tenors, yet one could see his point. She seemed a creature of another existence.

The coachman, now smiling as if drunk with the delights of his position, held open the door of the theatre and she floated through into the vestibule and looked around the motley collection assembled in the theatre at that time of day.

'Where is Herr Popper?' she asked in German – most heavenly of languages, most heavenly of voices! 'I wish to speak to the *schauspieldirektor*.'

The cloth-eared English gazed dumbly back, but I marched forward, overjoyed at the opportunity to speak – and *to this creature*! – in my own tongue.

'Let me take you to him, Madam.'

She turned and looked at me – a gaze instinct with feeling and intelligence.

'And you are? – no, let me guess. You are the great Wolfgang Gottlieb Mozart.'

I bowed humbly. Well, fairly humbly. The creature made me feel like a mere mortal in the presence of a goddess, but her words elevated me a few inches towards her own realm.

'I am honoured to make your acquaintance,' she said, giving me her hand to kiss. 'It was the prospect of singing your music under your direction that made me agree to Mr Popper's proposal. I reverence your genius.'

And she curtsied, tears in her eyes.

All this, of course, was lost on the mere English around. I was mortified that they could not understand her homage and would not believe it if I reported it to them later. When I reported it to them later. For here was understanding, here was appreciation! I gave her my arm.

'Mr Popper is I believe with Lord Hertford. Lord

49

Hertford is a patron of our Coronation season. Normally I would not interrupt them. But for Mme – am I not right in thinking it is Mme Hubermann-Cortino I am addressing?'

She nodded. 'Your servant, sir.'

'For Mme Hubermann-Cortino an exception must be made.'

We walked down the dingy corridor, I feeling ashamed of the inadequacies of my theatre, and I knocked on the door.

'Well, what is it?' came the tetchy voice. 'I am not to be disturbed.'

I opened the door and showed in the wonderful creature.

'Mr Popper? Mme Hubermann-Cortino.'

He started to his feet.

'But I didn't expect you – February at the earliest—' the creature burbled, making his incompetence immediately manifest. It was left to Lord Hertford to rise to the occasion.

'My dear Madam!'

He rose, then knelt at her feet and kissed her hand. It was a brave gesture for an elderly man, done creakily but with gallantry.

'Lord Hertford – Mme Hubermann-Cortino,' I murmured.

'Will you tell Lord Hertford,' she said, turning to me with an enslaving smile, 'that I am charmed and honoured to make his acquaintance. And of course Mr Popper too.'

Already she had Mr Popper's measure: she was treating him with contempt. Well, it saved time. Sopranos always treated impresarios with contempt before they had known them a week.

Mr Popper had regained a modicum of aplomb, and ushered her to a seat facing his desk. He now tried to rephrase his first question with more tact.

'My theatre is greatly honoured by your presence, my dear Madam. We had hardly dared hope for the pleasure and honour before the New Year at the earliest.'

When I had translated this she gave a scornful, operatic gesture with her elegantly-gloved hand.

'Vienna is insupportable! The opera houses riven with

dissension and jealousy. Politics, politics everywhere, and nowhere music! The thought of another Vienna winter, with the dreadful wind and snow, was too terrible to contemplate!'

So you have come to London, I thought. It hardly seemed the obvious choice. And there could be no work for her at the Queen's before the next March.

'And you are staying – where?' asked Lord Hertford.

'At the Fitzroy Hotel. My husband is at present seeking an apartment for us.'

'Your husband?' Lord Hertford could not forbear interrupting as I translated. She smiled regally.

'Yes, indeed, my husband. A former guardsman under Blücher. He acts as my manager, you understand. He has a little English, and will be seeking engagements for me in the months before the opera season.'

It occurred to me that the guardsman/manager had best take his wife with him when he went seeking engagements. But perhaps even that would be unnecessary. News of her would spread like wildfire, perhaps already had, hotel managers being what they were. A beautiful woman with a beautiful voice would always be in demand. The wonderful creature now added:

'Not that we need engagements. We have money enough. My purpose in coming here was to sing the music of the great Mozart with the advice and help of the composer himself.'

Suddenly I had two admirers, two disciples! Two beautiful women whose aim in life was to sing my music as it should be sung. When I translated this speech for Mr Popper he looked sceptical, as if he thought I was making it up.

'Well, we must start discussing the roles that you will sing next year,' he began. It was the wrong thing to say, from his point of view. The divine creature assumed it followed on from what she had just said.

'The Countess,' she immediately responded. 'I yearn to sing the Countess in *Figaro* under the direction of the genius who wrote it.'

Mr Popper, of course, immediately beat a hasty retreat.

51

'Oh, *Figaro, Figaro* . . . I don't see how. They did it at Covent Garden a couple of years ago.'

'With some of my arias and duets, none of my ensembles, and a great many songs by Mr Bishop,' I said acidly.

'But there you are, you see,' said Mr Popper with an ingratiating smile to Mme Hubermann-Cortino. 'People will say they've seen it. Composers are over-sensitive.'

'The man is a moron and a Philistine,' said the lady. I refrained from translating her. She stood up. 'I insist on singing the Countess in a production of Mr Mozart's *Figaro.*'

'Oh, ah . . . Well, er, if you *insist* . . . Perhaps if we did it with English dialogue . . .'

I felt I had been given backbone.

'Can you imagine this divine creature delivering English dialogue? It must be done with my recitatives in Italian.'

'Er, wouldn't that make it rather long?'

'Not a second longer than necessary.'

'Mr Popper, I think there is a way out of this,' said Lord Hertford, standing and asserting every inch his noble height. 'I shall pay for a new production of *The Marriage of Figaro*, with Mme Hubermann-Cortino as the Countess.'

'That is generous of you, My Lord,' said Mr Popper, ungracious as ever. 'But who will pay for the empty seats?'

But Mr Popper had forgotten who he was speaking to.

'Do you really imagine that with so divine a Countess there will be any empty seats?' asked Lord Hertford warmly. The implication that she would fill the theatre that my music would otherwise have emptied was not one I cared to look at closely. I have learnt to swallow insults and pocket the money.

'Very well then,' said Mr Popper, admitting defeat. '*Figaro* it shall be.' He turned to Mme Hubermann-Cortino and spoke loudly, as if to one of the inmates of Bedlam. 'I shall mount *Figaro* especially for you.'

His manner translated for him. Mme Hubermann-Cortino understood managers. She sailed to the door.

'Very well, then. All is arranged. We shall meet again. I must return to my husband.' She turned to Lord

Hertford. 'I am above all things grateful to you, My Lord, for your discrimination and great generosity. How can I ever repay you?'

She smiled enchantingly, floated down the dirty, peeling corridor and out into the vestibule without waiting for an answer. The number of people standing around had been augmented by later arrivals who had tarried there for a glimpse of so divine a creature. It would have been gracious of Mr Popper, fussing along in her wake, to introduce her to one or two of the people there. Needless to say he did not do so. At the door she turned.

'*Auf Wiedersehen*, then . . .' She ran her eyes over them, and her look alighted on Andrew Masters. She went over and graciously took his hand. 'You must be a singer. A tenor, perhaps?' The puppy-fat and air of self-love must have told her that. 'I hope I have the pleasure of singing with you.' Not in one of my operas, she won't! She returned to the door. 'Goodbye then, until we all meet again!'

And she sailed out, to be handed into the carriage by the besotted coachman. As the horses started up the Haymarket Lord Hertford and Mr Popper kept the coach in view as long as they could. Then Mr Popper turned and came over to me.

'Mr Mozart, you still have friends and relations in Austria?'

I was mystified.

'I have my dear sister Nannerl in Salzburg, and of course many musical friends in all parts of the country.'

He leaned forward, fixed me with his eye and hissed:

'Find out why she has left Vienna!'

CHAPTER SIX
La Finta Semplice

The writing of letters is no burden for me. It has been one of the solaces of my life, cut off as I have been from my own family, my own people, my own country. For me even a request for financial assistance can be a work of art, a small piece of drama, an aria without music. However, before I wrote to Nannerl as the despised Popper bade me, I composed a letter which I took no pleasure in, it being part of the fulfilment of the contract I saw myself as having entered into with Lady Hertford. I had to report to her, yet to give her as little real information as was consonant with our unspoken agreement. (It was a little bit like my policy when repaying monetary loans.) I imagined her prominent features furrowed in equine puzzlement as she read.

> The outlines of a splendid Coronation opera season begin to be clear. Mme Hubermann-Cortino has arrived from Vienna, and no one doubts the inevitability of a splendid success for her: she is loveliness itself, and has a voice of unparalleled richness and force. She is accompanied by her husband, a former guardsman.

(This last was in case she imagined Mme Hubermann-Cortino was likely to fall into the arms of my Lord Hertford, who, though elderly, is presumably still as susceptible as one of his cold disposition ever was.)

I have no doubt that with two sopranos of quality the season will be an extraordinary one, worthy of the patronage of His Majesty, and of the nobility and gentry. My own contribution, *Le Donne Giocose*, is all but completed, and in my humble opinion it is . . .

And so on, and so on. Self-praise is doubtless automatically suspect, but when it is the only sort available to one it is worth laying it on a bit.

By chance I had no sooner dispatched the letter than I encountered Mme Hubermann-Cortino in the Haymarket with her husband. She smiled at me enchantingly and introduced us. He is very tall and broad, with fearsome moustaches, but somewhat bloodshot of eye. If I were contemplating adultery (which Heaven forfend) I would weigh up the largeness of the person against the bloodshotness of the eye. His German was oddly accented, and I realised he must be of Italian-German origin – or was the Cortino of the name his alone? Was he an Italian who had fought as a mercenary in Blücher's army? Italians will fight for anyone, or pretend to. Their heels are at anybody's service. Not that he looked a coward, I have to admit. He looked much more like a bully.

'We now have a most convenient apartment in Bruton Street,' said his divine wife. 'You must come round of a morning to coach me in the role of the Countess.'

'My wife has the greatest respect for you as a musician,' said her bear of a husband, as if the gracious words had been taught him by rote. 'You will always be most welcome.'

I bowed. He bowed – with all the grace of an automaton. His enchanting wife smiled at us both.

'Do *please* come, dear Mr Mozart,' she said. 'With the proviso that on no account do you bring Mr Popper.'

'Mr Popper may have to be taught a lesson,' said the guardsman. I hastened to give them my assurance.

'There is no drawing-room to which I would take Mr Popper, Mme Hubermann-Cortino.'

'Therese. Call me Therese.'

Enchanting creature! Going on my way I puzzled over

her accent. German, but not a German that I knew. Not surprising, perhaps, since I have been cut off from my own lands – from the honour, fame and rewards that would inevitably have been mine – by the wars against the Corsican tyrant. I had travelled all too little in the land of heroes and true poetry, and my visit to Vienna in 1817 was alas ill-timed: the Emperor, whose father I had met as a child, was too preoccupied with affairs of state to grant me more than a public audience, and the Church dignitaries seemed to suspect me as tainted by English Protestantism – seemed, indeed, almost to regard me as an Englishman! But one thing I was sure of: the accent with which Therese spoke our native language was not that of Vienna.

That evening I wrote to Nannerl. My dear sister was wooed and won and carried back to her native land by an Austrian magistrate in 1784 to the great grief of our father and me (our mother was by then dead). Now a widow she lived – fortunate one – in beautiful Salzburg. After the usual report and jokes about the condition of my bowels I took up the matter of the divine Hubermann-Cortino. I did so, however, in as casual a manner as possible, not at all in the way of a spy requesting information. Some sort of inquisition into the details of the lady's life and private affairs was doubtless what the despicable Popper would have preferred. But such a creature was not a suitable subject for minute enquiry. She was as much above investigation as she was beyond reproach.

> The success of our opera season is now assured, for Therese Hubermann-Cortino has arrived among us, and I cannot doubt a stupendous triumph for her. She says she has left Vienna sickened by the quarrels and intrigues at the Opera. Sad indeed to hear that such conditions prevail at the home of lyric art! But no doubt the quarrelling is on *artistic* matters, not *personal* and sordid *financial* ones, such as is always the case in this island of blockheads. Do you know the causes of the dissensions there? They must be sorry indeed to lose the services of so divine an artist as she is. Apart from her career in Vienna I know nothing

of her. What other theatres has she sung in? Which princes have patronised her sublime art? Tell me what you know of her, that I may use it to spread her fame through polite London . . .

Her fame, in fact, spread without any aid from me. Lord Hertford was her first patron: she sang at a grand party in Hertford House, closely watched, I have no doubt, by Lady Hertford. She was invited to Chatsworth to sing for the Duke of Devonshire and a party there, and after that her success was assured. When she returned to London all that was necessary for her *louche* husband (why do divine women have such a fallibly human taste in men?) was to catalogue a list of engagements, public and private. When, on her free mornings, we studied the role of the Countess, her husband would sometimes loom in the door, listen for a minute or two with no sign on his face that he appreciated the ethereal beauty of what he was hearing, and then remove himself, allowing me at least to breathe more freely. These sessions at least taught me that the praise of her beautiful voice, which I so boldly inserted into my letters without ever actually having heard it, was amply justified, and that allied to the voice was solid technique and sensitive musicianship.

The news that Therese Hubermann-Cortino was to sing the Countess was received with admirable good humour by Betty Ackroyd.

'I am too young for it,' she said. 'Maybe in five or ten years' time I will be ready. Now the role of Susanna . . .'

Such generosity of spirit is seldom to be met with in the theatre. Betty would in fact have made an admirable Countess, but Therese was by far the more experienced artist. And Betty was still sufficiently light of voice to sing an enchanting Susanna. I called on her one day when I was not engaged to coach Therese. It was early for me, as I had been up betimes penning various letters of a financial nature. Resisting the temptations of Soho (the books and pamphlets on offer there from the peddlers are of a wretchedness and depravity beyond belief to one who respects, nay worships, Womankind), I threaded my way to her humble set of rooms, knowing that, it being a Wednesday, I would find her working with Bradley Hartshead. However as I quietly mounted the stairs it was not music I heard but speaking voices. I do not know what made me stop and listen – for I am not, believe me, one of nature's eavesdroppers – but it was probably the *accent* in which the words were spoken. I was hearing the voice of Betty Ackroyd, but it was speaking in the tones of a cockney slut.

'No m'Lord, I'm a good girl, I 'adn't done nuffing wrong wiv me boyfriend in the garden. I 'adn't done nuffing to be ashamed of at all.'

Then came the voice of Bradley Hartshead.

'Then why, my girl, were you skulking in the garden?'

'Cook is very strict. If she'd known as 'ow I went out of the 'ouse at night I'd've got me marching orders.'

'Will you tell me, then, what you claim to have heard as you were skulking in the garden?'

'Well . . . it's difficult, see, because I didn't understand . . . didn't understand what they was talking about.'

'Ah! And how *did* you come to understand?'

'Well, I told me boyfriend, and 'e . . .' The voice suddenly changed, becoming that of Betty Ackroyd. 'How *did* all this get out, Bradley? I mean, we ought to keep as close to the truth as possible. Did she tell her gardener boyfriend, and did he then sell the story to Frank?'

Frank! She called Lord Hertford Frank!

'I really don't know. We'd better ask him, I suppose. As you say, we ought to stick as close as possible to the truth. You're doing well so far, but you're still speaking up a bit too clearly, and not hesitating enough. Anyone who knew her wouldn't believe Jenny could do that.'

'I know. It's damned difficult being so inarticulate. But anyone who knew Jenny wouldn't believe she could say *anything* – in that setting, before those listeners. Oh, well, let's try again.'

But before she could resume her cockney voice I knocked on the door.

'Come in! Oh, Mr Mozart . . . You're earlier than we expected.'

Their confusion was palpable. I fear that mine was too. I muttered some muddled explanation and made my way to the piano. Betty was not dressed as Jenny, so there was no *éclaircissement* called for, but as Bradley slipped to sit beside me at the piano and Betty began to sing *'Deh vieni non tardar'* (perhaps my most beautiful melody!) it was clear that nothing was going to go right that day. Half-way through the aria Betty banged her hand on the top of the piano.

'You heard, didn't you?'

She was right as usual. We had to talk about it. I nodded my head miserably.

'I'm afraid so. I don't usually listen at doors. It was the voice, the accent: I heard it as I came up the stairs.'

'Where *can* we rehearse?' Betty demanded of Bradley Hartshead. 'Would the King lend us Buckingham House gardens?'

'Rehearse for the . . . trial?' I put in, knowing the answer. Everyone called it a trial, though it was only a sort of hearing. Betty's head went up and down vigorously, and now that her secret was shared she was smiling.

'Of course. Now you're the fourth person to know, and you have to keep absolutely quiet about it.'

'I don't have to ask why, I suppose?'

Betty laughed, her composure quite restored.

'Of course not. You can't imagine that poor slip of a thing testifying before the House of Lords, can you? I doubt they'd get a single word out of her. Someone has to tell the story for her, and this is the only way it can be done. Frank – Lord Hertford – knows all about my gifts as a mimic, and he approached me and asked me to do it.'

'And are you sure the story is true?'

She raised her eyebrows.

'Of course it's true. Lord Hertford would never risk its being found out if it was a lie.'

'But I heard you say – pardon me for overhearing – that you didn't know how the story had got to him.'

'Nor do I. But I'll find out. Obviously she talked, and whoever she talked to took the tale to him.'

'I suppose so,' I said, but still somewhat dubious. There

seemed a lot of assumptions here. 'Obviously the story will destroy the Queen entirely.'

'Oh, certainly. And the King will be very grateful. Lord and Lady Hertford too.'

'He's paying you for your services?'

'There will be a gift when the thing is done . . .' She smiled. 'A most munificent gift. Our fortunes – my fortune – will be made. I shall mention, of course, that you know and have been as silent as the grave.'

That seemed a little premature, and to smack of a bribe. But the circumstances of my life have made me eminently bribable. I nodded a solemn acceptance.

'Of course I shall tell nobody. Jeopardising hopes of the King's support for the opera season would be fatal at this stage. But aren't you afraid?'

'Afraid?'

'If the impersonation did get out it would ruin your prospects on the stage in this country. Support would immediately swing back to the Queen, and her personal riff-raff can be very violent. They simply would not suffer you to appear.'

'There are other countries to sing in. Anyway it won't get out.'

'Someone who knows Jenny could come to the hearing.'

'Her testimony – or mine, rather – will be a complete surprise, sprung at the last moment. And nobody knows her. I doubt even Alderman Wood or his wife would recognise her. Can you imagine her fellow-servants being at the House of Lords? Anyway, I shall *be* Jenny – Jenny with a voice.'

'Jenny does not *have* a voice, and anybody who knows her knows that too. If even a rumour got out there could be a danger that you would be . . . silenced.'

'Rumour will *not* get out. Now – "*Deh vieni—*" '

And she turned back to the aria, singing it this time like an angel.

In the days that followed (days in which I received answers to my requests for financial assistance that were far from satisfactory) I had to contend with growing doubts and fears. Lord Hertford appeared to be using his position as principal paymaster to the embryonic opera company to involve it in a project that was fraught with difficulties and dangers. In his commendable (well, fairly commendable) desire to help the King he was in danger of sailing beyond the windy side of the law and taking the company with him. That he was imperilling Betty Ackroyd's career, at least for the foreseeable future, was one important consideration. Still more important was the fact that he could be imperilling her life.

Those were the fears. The doubts nagged at me quite as insistently. From the moment I had heard Jenny Bowles tell her story – or have it told for her – I had wondered if it was the truth. The best argument I could come up with for its being true was that nobody would choose Jenny to tell a lie. But there were other questions too: how had her story come to Lord Hertford's ears? And what was his position in all this? He was husband to the King's principal mistress. There are doubtless some who gain pleasure from being cuckolded by royalty, but I would have expected them to come from the middle rather than the upper ranks of society. Could Lord Hertford really be such a man? He was, by all accounts, complaisant. But why should he be so eager to come to the King's assistance?

My state of mind was unenviable, and I was glad that I had more or less completed *Le Donne Giocose* or whatever I decided to call it, so that the atmosphere of good humour and forgiveness which pervades its final moments was not affected (though it must be said that I have lived a life of constant aggravation and privation and it has seldom, thank the Lord, affected my music). Alas, the reply from Nannerl when it came did nothing to restore my composure. After the usual jokes of a personal nature – *highly* personal, or rather personal at *bottom!* – she went on:

I had heard rumours concerning Mme Hubermann-Cortino's departure from Vienna even before I received your letter. No one has suggested that the departure was due to troubles at the Opera House, though certainly the usual intrigues and factions are at work there as ever. Mme Hubermann-Cortino sang there frequently in a variety of roles, and was well received by the Viennese public and aristocracy.

The rumour-mongers were busy, however, with her private life. The heir to the throne, the good Archduke Ferdinand, is as you know unmarried, and unkind tongues suggest that his mental capacity is limited. To be frank, some speak of him as close to an idiot. This would matter little in democratic Britain, where the King reigns but does not rule. But it matters here, where the Emperor rules (or employs Metternich to rule for him!). There is much talk of the Archduke marrying and producing an heir, or alternatively of his being deemed incapable of succeeding to the throne. His conduct is therefore constantly scanned.

How the affair began is a mystery. The Archduke is not known for his love of music. What everyone seems to agree about is that the Brunswicker's husband was far from outraged. Indeed it is said that the gallant soldier was the instigator, and had played the same role in other affairs of his wife with men of power and wealth. Truly we live in terrible times! How our good father would have been pained by such iniquity! But it must be said that affairs of the heart, including affairs with married women, are not unknown in the Imperial family. It seems, therefore, that there must have been some special reason for Prince Metternich bundling the Hubermann-Cortino woman and her scheming husband out of the capital and out of the country. But what it was the tongues of rumour disagree on. What they do agree on is that the precious pair will not be allowed back in a hurry . . .

I read the letter with outrage. Tongues of rumour indeed! I could believe *nothing* of what such tongues alleged against the divine Therese. Her purity and goodness were vouched for by her beauty and her excellent taste and principles. Clearly she had been the victim of the intrigues and libels of a rival soprano. I did not waver in my view that she was all a woman should be, and that she would be the foundation stone on which our glorious Coronation season of opera would be built (you see, I was beginning to suffer from the delusions of all those involved in operatic enterprises!).

But as I took a leisurely stroll in the direction of the Queen's Theatre I was assailed by the familiar nagging questions. If Therese had been bundled out of Vienna by Prince Metternich, why had she come so early to London? It was not the obvious place of refuge for a prima donna, particularly with our operatic life at such a low ebb. If Milan was ruled out by its Austrian rulers, why not Rome? Or Naples? Why not Munich or Berlin?

But those last names suggested a further train of thought, and I stopped in the vicinity of Carlton House and took out the letter to read it again, nagged by a half-memory. Yes – there it was! My dear sister referred to Therese as 'the Brunswicker'. So that explained the unfamiliar accent. And it gave me furiously to think. I had never heard that brand of German spoken before, but there would be many people in England who had. Because it was the German spoken by our own Queen, the wife of Prinny, Caroline of Brunswick.

CHAPTER SEVEN
Il Color di Morte

All this time the defenders of the Queen were testifying to her virtue before the House of Lords at Westminster. The fever pitch of partisanship had by now somewhat abated. People were bored with Caroline's pose of injured innocence. That she had been injured no one doubted, but fewer were now prepared to proclaim her innocence. Innocence, somehow, wore a different guise: it was not heavily rouged, it was not blowsy, it did not make gestures and strike poses that seemed to be aimed at the gallery. The gestures and poses seemed in any case to have been copied from the gestures of Italian opera singers – and provincial Italian opera singers at that. Attenders at the hearings were relieved when the Queen nodded off to sleep, which she rather frequently did.

I was much too busy to attend any of the hearings. Mr Clarkson had decided that one of the pieces that would fill in the time before rehearsals for the opera season could begin should be an old work of mine – *The Call to Arms*. It was a 'left-handed' piece, but one I am less indifferent to than most. It was based – very distantly – on Farquhar's *The Recruiting Officer*, so the libretto is less of a thin gruel than the books for the majority of such pieces. It was put together by some sorry hack whose name I forget who has since perished, I seem to remember, from war, pestilence, or want. Probably want. I wrote most of the music on the Continent in 1802, during the Peace of Amiens, and it is suffused with the joy and satisfaction of being at long last in Civilisation again. (The disappointments of the trip, financial and musical, as usual failed to intrude themselves into the music.) So that though most of the piece is pap, like all my English burlesques, there are one or two numbers such as the canon quartet of which I am not ashamed. I was quite looking forward to seeing it on stage again.

We had a fortnight for rehearsal and preparation – quite long enough if one went at it with a will. I recruited Bradley Hartshead to assist in the rehearsals and the training of the singers (insisting to Mr Popper that he be *paid*, which was agreed to with an ill grace). As rehearsals proceeded a certain buzz started going round the company, a feeling that this was a decidedly better offering than the Queen's standard article – not because any more money was to be spent on it than usual (of course not!) but because the music and the characterisation had a little more substance.

Betty was to play Marietta (I told you it was only *distantly* based on Farquhar). It was a good part with two quite attractive arias. I rehearsed her thoroughly, and quite often went to talk things over in her dressing-room. Brilliant creature that she is, she could both attend to my instructions and watch her dresser going about her acts of theatrical drudgery – ironing, ham-fistedly sewing, and helping on with costumes. There was about Jenny Bowles a slight access of confidence, a just perceptible lightening of the burden of dread. I surmised she had been told it would not be necessary for her to tell her story before the Lords tribunal.

The first night was scheduled for a day just as the Queen's defence was drawing to a close. Something of the players' anticipation of success had penetrated to the outside world. *The Call to Arms* had been popular when it was first played. It had coincided with the resumption of hostilities against the Corsican monster. However the war was so long-drawn-out, successes were so slow in coming, that patriotic fervour could not keep the audiences coming in for long. It was now fifteen years since it was last played, and people were regarding it as a new piece. All to the good. A fair sprinkling of the beau monde as it is called (inappropriately, considering their faces and figures) could be expected for the opening night.

By the time that occurred the cast was exceptionally well-drilled. We had some quite good singers even apart from Betty, and I had managed to get the tenor to sing and act as if the words and action actually had some meaning (though that would not last beyond the first few nights). When the opening night came I lingered round in the vestibule noting the notabilities: Lord Harewood, the Duke of Devonshire, the Duke of York (still in mourning for his wife, though only sartorially) – and of course my Lord Hertford, with his Lady. All these grandees acknowledged me most graciously, and some came over and shook my hand as fellow members of the Brotherhood. Lord Hertford, after acknowledging my presence, went over to have some words with Mr Popper, who was standing prominently in the centre of the vestibule, preening himself as if he had written the piece that was about to be performed. That left Lady Hertford alone. I should have made an early escape. My heart sank as, instead of talking to any of her fashionable friends, she advanced in my direction.

'Mr Mozart!'

In public rooms there was a slight whinny to her voice that was anything but attractive.

'My Lady.'

'We are expecting great things tonight.'

'Your Ladyship is too kind.'

'My husband says it is something special.'

I bowed. Her voice, to my relief, was lowered.

'I am grateful to you, Mr Mozart, for your letters.'

There was something in the voice – an edge – that alerted me to trouble coming.

'I have tried to keep Your Ladyship informed.'

'I am obliged to you for what you have told me. Less grateful for what you have *not* told me.'

'*Not* told you, My Lady?' I put on a pose of mock innocence. 'Of course I have not told you the gossip and small change of the day to day events in the company.'

My eye was most compellingly engaged by the spectacle

of her hand going into her reticule and coming out with a small purse.

'You mistook my purpose,' she said, her voice as unmusical as it could well be. 'I didn't want to hear gossip. I have no interest in who is pleasuring whom.' She leaned forward and hissed in my ear: 'I wanted to hear about money!'

I stared at her dumbfounded.

'I beg Your Ladyship's pardon—'

'I wanted – and want – to hear how much of his – and my – fortune My Lord is throwing away on this *opera* company'—there was such scorn in her voice!—'and on its singers.' Her eyes glinted: she was obviously on her favourite subject. 'Opera companies, as you must know as well as anybody, Mr Mozart, *eat up* money. I want to know how much my husband is throwing away. That was what I meant when I asked you to keep me informed of the arrangements.'

The purse transferred itself to my hand. It felt like a very small one. No doubt Lady Hertford felt she had already paid for information which she had not received. Now she retreated towards her natural friends, but before she reached them she turned her thoroughbred head in my direction.

'Write to me again, Mr Mozart!'

I stood there speechless. It must be said that Lady Hertford's reputation was not that of a generous or a charitable woman, though her independent fortune was large. In a word, she was thought to be rapacious, though rumour had it that the King was currently transferring his affections to a woman, Lady Conyngham, still more outrageous in her determined acquisitiveness. Truly such a man deserved to live in perpetual financial difficulties! I had not thought before, though, to question the gift of that purse. Clearly it had been intended by her as a sort of investment, to gain information on the expenditures of her less grasping husband.

Though to be sure Lord Hertford had never had the reputation of a generous man either. I had reason to be grateful to him, but in truth his expenditures were mostly in connection with his great love, music. His help to me had been timely rather than lavish. He knew (unlike his wife) when expenditure was called for from a man in his position. He was, in his rather old-fashioned way (for he was very much older than his wife) cultivated, suave, gentlemanly, but exceedingly cold. I would sooner petition him for money than for sympathy, but I would not expect a lavish amount of either. They were a couple, all things considered, from whom I would have preferred to keep my distance.

I turned to go backstage, but was prevented by the Brunswickian goddess and her more earth-bound husband.

'Mr Mozart! Our sincerest best wishes for success tonight.'

Talking to a true musician I was forced to dampen expectations. In fact the mere thought of her listening to one of my left-handed pieces was something of an embarrassment.

'Dear Madam – it is nothing. The slightest possible piece—'

'*Any*thing from the pen of Mozart *must* bear the stamp of genius.'

Her husband bowed and said something that seemed to be one of his routine and rote-learned compliments, but in the crush and babble it was quite incomprehensible.

I bowed, took one more look around the fairly glittering assembly, and disappeared back stage. There everything was in its usual state of hysteria and disorder. I will not bore you with the details. One tenor in a state of panic is very like another. The tenor this evening was Andrew Masters, and he was predictably fussing about autumn vapours (when was this god-forsaken city anything but vaporous?), the consequences for his voice, and his fears that he 'would not do justice to himself'. I told him I was sure he would reveal the full extent of his talents. You can tell he is a tenor, because he went away satisfied with that.

One oasis of calm and common sense was Betty Ackroyd. What is more she looked a picture.

'Your dresser is learning her trade,' I commented.

'I am my own dresser,' she replied. 'I have a washerwoman, a presser, a seamstress, but not a dresser.'

The chaos backstage was gradually reduced to manageable proportions by the efficient leadership of Edward Clarkson, and on a signal from him I went into the orchestra pit and took my seat at the fortepiano. Sometimes I go to my place unnoticed, but not tonight. Was I mistaken in feeling there was a particular warmth in the audience's response to my entrance? Probably. Most of these cloth-eared dullards I would guess did not know who I was, still less my connection with the piece that was to be played.

But there was no mistaking their enjoyment as the piece proceeded. They laughed and they clapped – could the author of a comic burlesque ask for more? In particular they applauded Betty Ackroyd, who from the start had them in the palm of her hand. Perhaps I was wrong in thinking that the burlesque was not for her – though it was not so much her voice or her musicality they cheered as her gifts for comedy and mimicry. I, sitting at the keyboard, filling in music that in truth needed no filling in, there mainly to direct the orchestra and singers, began musing on the dispensability of the continuo player, and wondering whether I wouldn't do better to go along with the Continental fad of waving a stick in front of the orchestra. It would certainly give me greater prominence. On the other hand Mr Popper would probably reduce my emoluments, on the grounds that I wasn't actually playing anything . . .

In the interval I went to the vestibule to mingle with the distinguished audience. This is something Mr Popper insists on, in the interests, so he says, of good relations with the public. I should have thought that providing them with good entertainment was the best way of procuring those. He was there once more himself, and a more ridiculous spectacle of turkey-cock conceit I could not imagine: he was, needless to say, taking credit for the success entirely to himself.

By chance I happened to bump into Lord Egremere and Mr Brownlett talking together. They were the two gentlemen, you will remember, who on the day of the old King's death had put the idea of a Coronation opera season into my head. They were profuse in their compliments on the performance and the music.

'A wonderfully happy evening,' said Lord Egremere urbanely. 'I had forgotten what a splendid little piece it was.'

I bowed my gratitude.

'And a splendid augury for the opera season next year,' said Mr Brownlett. 'Are arrangements coming along?'

'They progress,' I said cautiously. 'Money is a problem.'

Shutters went down on both their faces.

'It would be,' said Lord Egremere flatly. 'Country's in a parlous state.'

'It might be possible to acknowledge donations in the programme,' I suggested, turning to Mr Brownlett. ' "The opera season is put on with financial help from the Northern Counties Bank" – something like that.'

'Oh dear me no!' said Mr Brownlett, with something like panic in his voice. 'What would they say in Manchester or Leeds if they thought I'd been giving their money to an opera company? And a London one, at that!'

Ah well, another good idea whose time had not come. Their negative reactions made me doubly grateful for the support of Lord Hertford.

Lord Harewood passed by, with a young lady who was not his wife on his arm.

'Splendid little piece, Mr Mozart,' he said genially. 'Who wrote the music?'

It occurred to me to wonder whether Lord Harewood was not playing jokes on me.

My task of promoting good relations with the public done, I went backstage again. Betty Ackroyd was fuming because her second act dress had not been properly laid out for her. She looked glorious in it, however. Andrew Masters was fussing about whether he was doing justice to his vocal powers, and I said that all my expectations had been fulfilled. Then I went out and took my place once more at the keyboard.

The second half went quite as well as the first. This

70

London audience was beginning a love affair with Betty Ackroyd. At curtain call I was certainly not mistaken in detecting an increased warmth when I bowed by my instrument. But then a quite unaccustomed thing happened. Betty Ackroyd began pointedly applauding me from the stage. Most of the rest of the cast – my dear dunderheads of the Queen's Theatre's regular singers – followed suit, and then Betty came forward and beckoned me on to the stage. I disappeared into the bowels of the theatre, and a minute later appeared on stage, to gratifying applause. It was like the first night of *Figaro* come again. Now I in my turn applauded the cast and then modestly made my way to the wings.

'Mr Mozart!'

It was Mr Popper, red and bulging of eye, calling me over. I thought he must be annoyed with me for taking a curtain call on stage. I was just about to go over to him, with considerably more confidence than I usually carried to recriminatory sessions with him, when Betty came off and took me back on to the stage to renewed applause. Again as I came off there was Mr Popper, standing in the shadowy depths of the wings, and beckoning agitatedly.

'Mr Mozart! Quick. Come with me immediately. There is no time to lose!'

Bemused I followed him. Back through the dusty wings, down dim corridors, up stairs.

'I don't understand,' I said. 'Why are you not enjoying the applause? It's been a great success!'

Mr Popper shook his head with gloomy significance and put his finger to his lips. This drew my attention to his hands. They were shaking. This was not to be a ritual dressing down, a dampening of expectations such as singers and composers regularly receive from opera managers, and authors, I am told, from their publishers. Something had occurred that had terrified Mr Popper.

We were at last in the long corridor on the first floor where most of the company's dressing-rooms were. Further and further we went. What could this mean? At last he stopped outside Betty Ackroyd's room.

'Prepare yourself, Mr Mozart.'

Foolish thing to say! How can you prepare yourself for you-know-not-what? For one moment the awful prospect of harm having come to Betty Ackroyd flooded into my mind, the very harm I had feared, but then I shook myself: I had just left her on stage, acknowledging applause. I swallowed. Mr Popper opened the door and I went in.

The first thing I saw was Lord Hertford, standing, but leaning heavily on a stick, looking years older than when I had greeted him earlier in the evening. He looked at us, and then looked down. At his feet, her head facing away from us, sprawled into a curling shape around a little table, was a woman. She was wearing the usual drab dress of Jenny Bowles, but in its back there was a hideous red gash – a gaping wound from which the weapon had been wrenched. I remember giving a little desolate whimper of distress for the poor, sad creature.

'Is it – it is Jenny, isn't it?'

'Yes,' said Lord Hertford.

'And there's no question she is—?'

'Dead, Mr Mozart.'

'No question?'

'No question at all. That is how Mr Popper found her.'

I moved forward. I came round to the other side of the table and looked down at her face. Words of my dear, improvident friend da Ponte came into my head: '*quel volto tinto e coperto del color di morte.*' The death of the Commendatore in Act I of *Giovanni*. And here was this sad scrap of humanity at my feet. The powerful, dignified paterfamilias, the pathetic creature who could hardly string two words together, yet for both the 'colour of death' was the same. My heart turned over for her. I looked towards Lord Hertford and Mr Popper.

'Now, how are we going to dispose of the body?' asked Lord Hertford.

CHAPTER EIGHT
Trial by Water

I spluttered. I'm afraid I splutter more and more as I get older, when I am surprised, or, as now, when I am outraged. As a younger man I took things more in my stride (and there were many things, believe me, to take).

'But surely we must fetch a magistrate—'

'My dear Mr Mozart, she can't be found here,' said Lord Hertford, seeming to summon reserves of resilience. 'A former servant at Alderman Wood's house, found dead in a theatre with which I am associated? No, no, she can't be found here. In fact, for a variety of reasons, I don't think she can be found at all.'

There were sounds of footfalls down the corridor. The curtain calls were over.

'Mr Popper, slip outside and prepare Miss Ackroyd – quietly and tactfully.' That last word gave him cause to reconsider. 'No – on second thoughts you go, Mr Mozart. Betty will have to know. Warn her before she comes in, in case she screams.'

As I turned to the door it crossed my mind that in that instant, in going along with their plan, I was probably compounding a felony or committing some other high-sounding crime. I wondered whether I could plead ignorance of the law, on the grounds of not being a British subject. It seemed unlikely, in view of the fact that I have been in the country since I was seven. I would just have to plead the truth: that I am accustomed, when told to do something by a person of title, to do it.

Betty Ackroyd was coming along from the stairs, happy

and excited, with other members of the cast. One by one they turned into their own dressing-rooms until she alone was left. She saw at once from my face that something was amiss.

'Prepare yourself for something very unpleasant,' I said. 'On no account should you scream.'

She looked up at me for an instant, then swallowed. I opened the door and she passed in. I followed and shut the door behind us. Betty looked down at the terrible yet pathetic sight on the floor of her dressing-room.

'Oh no! Poor damned child . . . Poor, poor Jenny!'

She seemed about to bend over her, but Lord Hertford put up his hand and stopped her.

'No point in going close. She's quite dead, I'm afraid. Now, the question is: what to do next?'

'We have to get rid of the body,' said Betty at once.

'Of course. You must have nothing to do with that. Go into the corner there and change into your day dress. We three will look the other way. Should be screens here, Mr Popper. Then you must leave and go home with Bradley in the usual way.'

She looked at him, then nodded, and with her usual self-possession and quiet efficiency she went to the corner where her day dress hung, and began to unlace herself. I of course turned away, as Lord Hertford had promised. My mind was racing. I was shocked that Betty had immediately gone along with – nay, had independently suggested – the proposed illegal disposal of poor Jenny's corpse. What was it intended we should do? Take the body to Regent's Park or Hyde Park, to be found by a park-keeper in the morning? Leave her in Soho, and hope that the Runner or Watchman who found her would draw the obvious conclusion? But what if she had not lost her virtue?

'Right,' said Betty, her voice cracking as it had never cracked during her performance. 'People may wonder why I have gone home after a success like this. . .'

'Then stay around in the vestibule for a little while, particularly if there are patrons still there. When you do go, you will find Tom my coachman waiting in the

Haymarket. My Lady will have gone in her own coach, thank heavens. Tell Tom to come up here, but *discreetly*.'

And so we three stood there, waiting, listening to the sound of the actors one by one departing, with their usual actorish greetings. We had locked the door, so we had no fear of being surprised. After a while Lord Hertford sank down on the threadbare old sofa, looking quite exhausted, but none the less deep in thought. Finally he spoke to Mr Popper.

'The theatre should be emptying by now. Go down and tell your people that you have work to do, caused by the immense success of the piece. Tell them you will leave by the stage door and lock it up. That is the best way for us to leave too, when the time comes.' As the impresario went to the door he asked suddenly: 'Got a coffin, Mr Popper?'

Popper started.

'A coffin? Oh, I see: a stage property.' He posed, as if in thought. 'No, I can't say we have. We specialise in comedies. There's been no call. Would a travelling trunk do?'

'Admirably. It's sturdy, is it?'

'Sturdy enough for her.'

He was about to slip out when there was a knock at the door. Lord Hertford got painfully up, opened it, and let Mr Popper out. As his steps faded down the corridor he pulled inside the door his hefty coachman. The man smelt of beer and onions, and his eyes popped out when he saw Jenny.

'Tom, we have to get rid of *that*.'

'I can see that, My Lord.'

He didn't turn a hair. It was as if getting rid of bodies was all in a day's work for him. They went into a whispering huddle and I didn't try to hear what was said. I hoped my part in the business was at an end and that I would be allowed to go back to my rooms and forget the horror of it in a pint of sherry and sleep. Then I caught My Lord looking in my direction as he spoke, then back to his coachman. No such luck: I was going to be involved, whether I liked it or not. I had been in on the matter since Jenny appeared on the scene, and I was going to be in on it till – somehow or other – she disappeared. Why me? I thought. I had nothing against Queen Caroline, beyond the fact that she was vulgar, without taste, promiscuous and probably not in her right mind. And the same could be said of several of the King's brothers.

Tom departed with a little bow. Lord Hertford shut the door, locked it, then walked heavily back to the sofa and sank into it.

'Nothing to do but wait,' he said. I cleared my throat.

'When do you think we can . . . set about it?' I asked. He took a jewelled gold watch from his waistcoat.

'I should think we might get started about half-past eleven,' he said. 'With precaution, naturally. It will have to be absolutely quiet in the Haymarket, but once we've got her on to the coach we should be all right.'

'And where?—' I began, but was interrupted by a knock at the door. Lord Hertford handed me the key.

'It will be Tom.'

It was, with a box over his shoulder. It wasn't a very large box, but then Jenny Bowles hadn't been a very large person. It was a tatty job, put together by the theatre's carpenter, and it was crudely painted, with the name 'Peter' on the front. I vaguely remembered its being used in a piece called *The Jolly Tar*, when the hero went off to sea with his belongings. I forget whether I wrote the music or not, but I do recall sitting at the harpsichord night after night, watching the witless action. It was about the time of Nelson's victories, and people were much taken up with matters naval. The quality of the piece was immaterial, which was lucky.

Tom came in, and lowered the box by the gruesome corpse on the floor. Lord Hertford nodded to me – ME! – to help him put poor Jenny into her coffin. I gave him a look he couldn't ignore.

'If you would be so good, Mr Mozart.'

There are moments when I refuse to be taken for granted. I nodded my agreement and bent over. Tom could in fact have shovelled her in single-handed, but we did it a little more reverently. He took the head and I took the ankles, and together we lifted the body up – light as a

76

cat's, it seemed – and then down into the box. Thankfully I shut the lid.

'Couldn't we take it down to the stage door?' I asked, anxious to get it out of the room. Lord Hertford pondered.

'Better not. One of the watchmen could come round. It's safer here. We could hide it under the dressing table if necessary.'

He seemed unmoved by the makeshift coffin's presence. He had apparently regained some of his vigour, and his eyes glinted keenly as he thought the matter through. After a minute or two he beckoned Tom over.

'Putney, I think, as you suggested,' he said. 'Putney would be best.'

They had obviously discussed various possibilities when they had their muttered discussion at the door, and now Lord Hertford had come to a decision. My heart sank. Putney seemed a hundred miles away. My night was going to stretch into day. My Lord tapped his watch.

'Go and make everything ready, Tom, and come back at half-past eleven.'

Tom bowed and left again. I locked the door. So there we were, the two of us, a happy little party, Lord Hertford saying nothing and me quaking with apprehension. Where Mr Popper was I did not know, but I suspected in his office with a bottle for company. His drink was gin – a typically low preference. Still, I would have been happy with a bottle of anything at that moment. I looked around me but could spy none. Betty Ackroyd had clearly no need of the sort of stimulant many actresses and singers need before a performance. It would come, I thought, as the years of makeshift, setbacks and disappointments which is the lot of the English stage player took their toll on her optimism.

The minutes ticked by, with none of the speed they ran with for Faust awaiting midnight. (Faust – now there's a subject for an opera. Just the subject for an old man!) I walked restlessly up and down, but a look shot from under Lord Hertford's elegantly-trimmed eyebrows told me I was distracting his train of thought. I sat at Betty's dressing table and began jotting down the first movement of a serenade for wind instruments that I had had in my mind for some days. Suitable music for an aristocratic rout in Coronation Week. I do sometimes wonder why the aristocracy requires *new* music for such occasions, when no one listens anyway. But of course for me the first requirement is that they *pay*.

At last it came. There was a knock on the door, I let Tom in, and at a nod from Lord Hertford we went over to the makeshift coffin.

'Where's Mr Popper?' asked Lord Hertford.

'At the stage door,' said Tom, 'keeping a lookout.'

I detected a too-readiness about the answer. There was something wrong and I could guess what it was.

Through the door we manoeuvred the box, then along the long corridor and down the stairs. It was no great labour, because it was so sadly light, but I resented my being expected to do menial work, as I resented being caught up in a criminal enterprise without so much as a question as to whether I consented or not. When at last we got to the stage door Mr Popper was standing there, red of nose, glassy of eye, the shape of a flask very visible through his coat pocket.

'Got her there, have you?' he said thickly. 'Got *it* there, I should shay.'

As Lord Hertford approached behind us he elaborately opened the door, took a step out into the little side-alley, and came back in. He stood swaying by the door.

'Shilent as the grave,' he said.

He clutched at the door-post to steady himself.

'The man's drunk,' said Lord Hertford disgustedly. 'Go back to your office, for heaven's sake. You'll be more danger than help. Tom, go out to the Haymarket and see that it really is quiet. And open the door to the carriage.'

Mr Popper swayed off without another word. After he had turned the corner his footsteps became more certain and confident. He was, I suspected, drunk, but not so drunk as he pretended. The cunning rascal! He had got himself out of the most dangerous (and criminal) part of the enterprise!

Tom slipped back in through the door.

'All clear, My Lord. Not a sparrer stirring.'

'All right. Now *quickly*, and quietly too.'

We lifted the box, scuttled out through the door held open for us by Lord Hertford, then down the murky little passageway, out into the street, and quick as a flash in through the coach door with the box. Lord Hertford was immediately behind us, and he pushed me, very loath, into the coach and onto the seat facing the driver and facing the coffin. He then climbed in and sat beside me.

'Right and away, Tom,' he said. 'Keep a steady pace – don't want to attract attention.'

The coach had to turn in the street. The box lurched at the turn, and I had to put my hand over to steady it. It was one of Lord Hertford's pokiest and least stately coaches (no doubt Tom had sent back for it at His Lordship's command, so that we should be inconspicuous) and he and I were crammed together on the seat, unable to avoid undignified contact. It produced, however, no feeling of intimacy between us. Lord Hertford was deep in thought, and I was deep in fear. I was also very, very uncomfortable. It must have been a coach reserved for exceedingly poor relations.

The journey seemed endless, and was indeed very long. By the time we were trundling through the narrow streets around Westminster I was already feeling that Tom was overdoing the steady pace. By Chelsea I felt like screaming with frustration. If I was to be involved in a criminal action I wanted it over and done with as soon as possible. I suppose that means I would make a bad criminal. My Lord just sat there, chin in chest, sighing from time to time, thinking things through. My Lord was always, I now realised, prepared for everything – the least spontaneous of men. Well, perhaps it was as well for one of us to be like that.

Finally, after what felt like hours and hours of travel, we seemed to be in Putney. I knew something of the village, having once lodged there during a period of greater than usual financial stringency. In fact I was glad it was not daylight, for reasons I need not go into. Tom went on, through the High Street, then down towards the river, obviously knowing exactly where he was going. Where *were* we going, I wondered?

The answer came quite soon. We stopped by the riverside, in a lane used by poor travellers who wanted to take a boat across. There was not a light on the shore, but we could see a little from the shimmering moonlight on the Thames. Tom jumped down briskly, then helped us down, both of us very stiff from the rattling of the carriage and the ill-padded seats. Tom then jumped into the carriage and took hold of the far end of the coffin.

'If you could take the other hend, Mr Mozart. . .'

I sighed inaudibly and took hold of it. In no time the light burden of poor dead Jenny was laid down on the soil. Tom, nippily for a heavy man, reached beside the coachman's seat and brought down a length of rope and a heavy block of iron, doubtless something that had its use in the routines of the stable, perhaps a mounting block for children. He put the rope and heavy weight on top of the coffin.

'Now, no need for you to come, My Lord,' he said, with the brisk familiarity of an old servant. 'In fact, I'd hadvise you to walk about a bit, so long as you keep us in view and are back 'ere when we're back. Don't want you to be hassociated with this 'ere desperate henterprise.'

Oh no! We can't have the prime mover and instigator involved! He must be kept out of it by every means possible. Whatever happened to *noblesse oblige*, I wondered? It seems to be the poor old common man who does all the obliging these days.

As Lord Hertford nodded his ready agreement we bent down and picked up the box by its handles. It was now much heavier by reason of the weight that was to take Jenny down to the watery depths. There was a wharf just below the path, and, painfully twisted round to make sure of my step, I backed uncertainly down towards it. When, at some point, I turned my head forwards, I saw Lord Hertford walking with apparent nonchalance away from the carriage.

'Right!' said Tom, when we were down on the wharf. We

put the box down and he dusted his hands. 'There she is,' he said, and pointed to one of three or four flat-bottomed craft moored by the side.

'But we can't just—' I began.

'Me bruvver's,' said Tom succinctly. ' 'Ere, let's get the little lady on board.'

When we had laid the box on the bottom of the punt, Tom opened the lid and without emotion took the body out. I didn't offer to help him.

'I suppose you couldn't tie this 'ere block to the body while I get the punt under way, could you?' he asked.

'I don't think I'd be much good—' I began.

'Didn't think so,' he said, as if oddly pleased. He had only asked me to emphasise his own physical prowess and hardness of character. 'Some sort of fiddler, aren't you? Mustn't 'arm those 'ands.' He tied the rope securely round the heavy block, then attached it to the body. 'That'll do the trick,' he said. Then he unmoored the punt, took up the long pole, and we made towards the deepest part of the river.

'You're an expert,' I said, rather ridiculously making conversation.

'Done it all me life,' he said, nodding complacently. 'Would 'a gone on the river like me bruvver, but I prefer 'orses.'

In no time we were in the middle of the dully gleaming waterway. Tom put the pole carefully along the bottom of the boat, then, without even bothering to ask for my help he took the body of Jenny in his arms, straightened, and threw it into the water. It lay on the surface for just a second, then sank down with a sinister gurgle. Tom bent down, took up the box, then tore it apart and threw it into the river to augment the driftwood there. He didn't wait to watch, but took hold of the pole again and we began back towards the shore. He could have been disposing of bodies in the Thames all his life. The thought discomposed me. I shivered.

As he tied up the vessel I made my way up the wharf and back to the coach. Lord Hertford was approaching it from another direction, and I waited respectfully by it. He climbed in and I climbed in after him. In a matter of seconds we felt Tom climb on to the driver's seat, crack his whip, and start the long journey back to London.

It was almost as silent as the journey out had been. Lord Hertford asked no questions, assuming the thing had been done as he must have directed. As we were going through Chelsea I started. He looked at me enquiringly.

'I've just realised I didn't say a prayer for the poor girl.'

I could only dimly see his face, but I think its expression became quizzical, and an eyebrow was raised. That, at least, was how I imagined his reaction. I shut my eyes and said a silent prayer. Half an hour later Lord Hertford, struck by I know not what thought, said: 'I'm obliged to you, Mr Mozart.' I merely inclined my head and said 'My Lord.' It would have been ridiculous to say 'Not at all.'

We were by then going through Westminster. It became apparent that we were not going to put me down at my apartment, but were headed for Lord Hertford's town house in Manchester Square. I said nothing. It was not my place, and I was wondering if he intended to show his appreciation as we parted. As we pulled up outside the magnificent edifice and a sleepy footman opened the door Lord Hertford, helped down by Tom, turned towards me.

'Tom will drive you to wherever you live, Mr Mozart.'

I shook my head and climbed out after him.

'I fancy a walk and some night air, My Lord.'

'As you please, Mr Mozart.' He shook my hand with the first real appearance of warmth and gratitude. 'You must call on me, Mr Mozart, whenever I can be of service to you.'

I cleared my throat.

'I regret to say, My Lord, that I am rather in need of pecuniary assistance at this moment.'

'Very well, then. Come and see my steward in a day or two's time.' It was spoken readily, but there was something in his manner – a perceptible diminution of warmth and gratitude – that suggested he would have preferred to be of service to me in some other way. I was well acquainted with rich men feeling like that. But this time he would surely feel obliged to be generous. He was about to go into his house, but turned back.

'You have done me – and the King – great service. The testimony can now be given as planned.'

I started.

'The testimony?'

He raised his eyebrows.

'Of course. The testimony before the House of Lords. What else did you suppose this was about?'

And at last he went in, and the door was shut behind him. Tom drove off round to the mews, and I was left to walk home with more than enough to think about as dawn began to show dimly and reluctantly on the horizon.

CHAPTER NINE
Masetto

I awoke well after midday, moderately refreshed in body but fearful in spirit. The night before I had drunk a pint of claret and eaten a wedge of game pie I had found in the larder, the freshness of which was suspect. I was pleased to see from my motions that my digestive system did not seem to have suffered. I sent out for ham and beef to breakfast on, putting thought from me. When I was replete I jotted down some ideas for the little wind serenade and began working them out. Like Macbeth I knew that to think of some things leads surely to madness. One of the lessons I have learnt in my life is to step on from difficulties, embarrassments, disasters, and to live the next day as if nothing had happened.

I received that day a letter from my son Charles Thomas, pressing me to visit him in Wakefield, where he teaches music in Miss Mangnall's school, as well as to the cream of the town's citizenry. It was tempting indeed: to escape from the perils and uncertainties of my present life in London to rural (well, fairly rural) simplicities. But first there were things to be done: I had to direct the early performances of *The Call to Arms*, ensure that the preparations for *two* of my own operas were in train, and collect my money from Lord Hertford's steward.

And I was due at the Queen's that night for the second performance. That was inevitable, but how readily I would have avoided going back to that place! To work up the spirit needed to walk in there as if nothing had happened I decided to have a hearty dinner at Mr Benbow's Chop House in the Strand.

Mr Benbow, however, thought otherwise. As I walked in he intercepted me, bustling up self-importantly, with all the cares of a chop house bowing his shoulders, and pushing aside the friendly waiter who was leading me to a table.

'Mr Mozart, I'm afraid—'

'Never fear!' I said confidently. 'I have expectations of generous help from Lord Hertford tomorrow.'

'Mr Mozart, when do you *not* 'ave expectations?'

'These expectations are based on—' I paused. How to phrase it so as to give nothing away? 'These expectations are based on very considerable services rendered.'

'When are they not, Mr Mozart?' He repeated his question with an almost sadistic insistence, and drove home his advantage. 'But 'ow often are they fulfilled? And if by any chance they were, what warranty is there that I should see any of the money? I seldom 'ave in the past. Your bill is as long as my arm.'

I was forced back on my usual solution.

'Anyone written poems for you recently, Mr Benbow? Poems on the succulence of your chops, or the . . . er . . . delightful qualities of your daughter?' This was Mr Benbow's weak spot – a fondness for his daughter, combined with one for tenth-rate art. Any hack writer could earn himself a meal, or at least stave off the bailiffs. 'I could set it to music.'

He stopped, irresolute.

'Well, there *was* a very pretty set, written by a young man from 'ampstead a few months back. *Two* verses, and they flowed something beautiful. About my daughter Molly they were . . . I could do you the fish and a guinea fowl.'

'And a bottle of hock.'

'Oh dear, Mr Mozart,' he sighed. 'You drive a hard bargain for one who 'asn't a penny in the world.'

'It's those who haven't a penny in the world who need to drive hard bargains,' I said, as we threaded our way through to an obscure table much too near the kitchens.

So there I was, eating moderately well, though drinking the dregs of some justly infamous German vineyard. The poem was a pretty piece of nothing by one of the cockney friends of Leigh Hunt, and I had set it with my left hand before the fish arrived, giving the second verse enough twiddles and twirls to make it look different from the first. Then I ate heartily and thought.

First I went over in my mind the whole of Jenny Bowles's brief and disastrous association with the Queen's Theatre. I came reluctantly to the conclusion that Jenny's story was true (subject to the proviso that she could have misunderstood what she heard). To believe otherwise seemed to present too many difficulties. My Lord Hertford was not, I suspected, above suborning one of Alderman Wood's servants to tell a false tale at the Queen's trial. But he would not in that case suborn the least likely, least vocal, least convincing of his household staff – one who, it turned out, was all but useless. The inference was inescapable: Jenny had heard what she said she had heard, and had gone to Lord Hertford with it. Or had she discussed it with someone first? Alderman Wood's cook or butler? Her lover perhaps? And had Lord Hertford thought of that possibility?

In any case, as soon as Lord Hertford was informed he had seen the chance to scupper the Queen and ruin her reputation for ever. Part of the Queen's appeal, even if this was seldom put into words, was that if she had behaved badly Prinny had behaved worse. That appeal would be destroyed if Jenny's story got out.

So Jenny had been concealed at the theatre, given a plausible occupation there, ate and slept there. At some stage Lord Hertford had realised that she could never testify before the House of Lords, and had taken ingenious steps to arrange a substitute for her. *That*, at any rate, seems to have remained a secret, at least from whoever it was who still thought Jenny worth killing. But Jenny's important role in this high matter of state *must* have got out: otherwise why would she now be lying on the bottom of the Thames?

As the waiter with barely-concealed contempt removed the remains of my fish a terrible thought struck me: if the proposed substitution for Jenny had got out, it might be Betty Ackroyd lying now on the bottom of the Thames. It was a terrible sin to consider that one of God's creatures was more easily dispensed with than another, both of them young women with their lives ahead of them, and I rebuked myself. But the thought remained: Betty could be the one the fishes were now feeding on.

I went over in my mind the events of the night before. Among the people who most obviously might have killed Jenny were all the cast, all their helpers, and what is humorously termed the management of the theatre: Mr Popper and his underlings. Then there were the fine folk in the audience – Lady Hertford and her friends, Lord Harewood, the bankers and money-lenders and all the rest. There were also the artistic people – the Hubermann-Cortinos among others. Anyone from these various groups could have slipped backstage at the interval. Lady Hertford had been known to go behind the scenes with her husband (though she had not been welcome and she had not been pleasant). Then there was Lord Hertford himself . . . The picture came to my mind of him bending over the body.

But what did he have to gain by Jenny's death? On the surface he had a great deal to lose.

Had Jenny been alive at interval time? I remembered Betty Ackroyd complaining that her second act costume had not been ironed. But Betty could hardly have failed to notice a body in the middle of her dressing-room floor. Had she seen Jenny at interval time? If so, what had been her state of mind? If not, where had she been, and had she been alive or dead?

These reflections, with related speculations and fantasies, kept my mind occupied throughout the consumption of a guinea-fowl that was stringier than a guinea-fowl has a right to be. It occurred to me that when Lord Hertford's steward stumped up with the handsome present it might be sensible to give Mr Benbow something substantial on account. The trouble is, when it comes to the point, I very seldom do the things that it would be sensible to do.

I had thought the matter over and had decided not to go and see the Hertfords' steward that day. Too importunate by half. So when I had finished my meal I dispatched a note by a street urchin whom I have often used in emergencies, fixing the next day as the time when I would wait on him. Then I left the chop house (without a word of thanks or appreciation from Mr Benbow) and began the walk towards the Queen's Theatre. It was as I was walking down Cockspur Street that a further thought occurred to me.

In the dressing-room, as we all stood round the terrible thing on the floor, Lord Hertford had told Betty Ackroyd to go home with Bradley as usual. I had registered at the time, but had put the thought from me as more pressing matters elbowed it out. But what did he mean? That Bradley usually escorted Betty home after the performance? I confess it *sounded* more than that – more as if they were living together. I had been many times in Betty's humble apartment in Soho, and Bradley had more often than not been there, but I had never gained the impression that they were together there, cohabiting, as the law puts it, or even that they were lovers. Am I simply unsuspicious by nature? I must say that I had never seen beyond the small sitting-room, which the fortepiano rendered even smaller. About the sleeping arrangements if any I had no notion, and of course had made no enquiries.

The audience were arriving for the performance as I reached the Queen's. There was none of the smartness and style of a first-night audience: second nights are notoriously prone to accidents and lethargy. This was an audience of townsfolk and their wives, and their arrival was watched by no more than a single yokel on the opposite pavement. There was nothing to be gained by mingling with them, so I went at once back stage.

I had realised, of course, that nothing could be said about the events of the night before. Still, I was a little surprised when I bumped into Mr Popper and he merely said: 'Keep them on their toes tonight, Mr Mozart. We can't have slackness setting in.' It was as if the night before had been a first night like any other. Surely some *look* – of sympathy, complicity, *something* – would have been more appropriate, and would have acknowledged my leading role in the events, if not his own dismal showing? But Mr Popper is a man totally without tact, consideration or human feeling – the typical opera manager, in fact. He once, I remember, brought me a piece by Salieri and said it was a little heavy for English taste and I was just the man to adapt it! Of course I refused. Salieri has always been most courteous to me in our communications, so who was I to insult him by watering down his charming little score? It was only later, in one of my dire financial emergencies, that I was forced to do what the appalling Popper asked of me.

As I did for the performance that night, admonishing the players and singers, spurring them on, securing a performance which (apart from Betty Ackroyd's being slightly out of voice) was hardly inferior to that of the night before. The audience of beef-witted Britons enjoyed themselves in their way, though of course every joke had to be underlined, shouted loud, repeated two or three times before they could see the point. I dream that one day I will see one of my *real* operas – the divine *Così* perhaps – performed by Germans before a German audience, one sophisticated enough to appreciate subtlety, understand the jokes the first time, not to need the cleverness underlined by horseplay and vulgar fooling.

Backstage the actors were buoyed up by the piece's success. Many of them had gone to a nearby tavern the night before, and asked me where I had been. I pretended I had been overcome by my old piece's new-found popular favour – as if it were one of my *real* works! – and had gone home. Betty Ackroyd was worried about her voice, and was doing all the superstitious rather than medical things that singers do do when they are a little hoarse. She was fast becoming a professional! She looked at me and raised her eyebrows, but beyond that she gave no indication that the day before had been anything other than an ordinary day in the theatre.

A joke was going round backstage during the interval, a joke that the Queen had made. 'Yes, it is true I have committed adultery – *once*,' she was reported to have said. 'It was with the husband of Mrs Fitzherbert.' It went from mouth to mouth, with roars of laughter at each retelling. It would not have been so if Lord Hertford had been around. In his presence Caroline was always called 'the Princess', and any joke would have to be at her expense, not at her fat husband's. I refrained from pointing out that the Queen had never been known to make a good joke before, and if she did so now it obviously had been fed to her by one of her entourage, probably that clever villain Brougham. But at least it was a good joke.

After the performance I collected together my music and made my way out to the Haymarket with the utmost dispatch. The theatre did not *feel* good, if I may so express it: it did not seem right to be there knowing what I knew yet unable to talk to anyone about it. The shadow of Jenny, who had been so wraith-like even in life, lingered around the back-stage areas. The last of the audience were straggling out into the street as I quitted the place, and I registered the yokel still watching them. I felt a twinge of disquiet, but was diverted by a call from the theatre.

'Mr Mozart!' It was one of the doormen, a man hired for his height rather than his brains. He was holding a pair of spectacles in large, clumsy hands. 'Is these yours, sir? They was found on the pie-*ann*-o.'

I took them, nodded my thanks and went on my way. But I had no sooner plunged into the murk of Orange Street than I heard quickened steps coming up behind me, then a shadow appearing at my shoulder. My first thought was that I was being robbed. Luckily, as usual, I had almost nothing on me.

'Mr Mozart!'

A cultivated robber, a burglarous music-lover! But of course I had been identified by the blockhead of a doorman. There was no point in hurrying on. I turned with reluctance.

'Mr Mozart, could I have a few words with you?'

It was the country boy I had seen watching the theatre. I was seized with foreboding. Not that there was anything alarming about the boy himself. He was rather below middle height – his eyes, in fact, looked straight into mine – a square, tanned, attractive face and a square body, roughly but neatly dressed. At once I lost my fears of being robbed, but replaced them with other fears.

'Yes?'

'It's about Jenny, sir. Jenny Bowles.'

My forebodings were realised. I knew at once who the boy was. I temporised.

'Would you mind if we went back into the Haymarket? There's a little more light there. Talking to people in darkness always makes me nervous.'

' 'Twasn't my intention to do that, sir,' the young man said. 'I thought if I followed you all the way home you might think you was goin' to be robbed.'

'I might, I might.' We were back into the broad spaces of the Haymarket, and I got a better view of his strong, anxious face. 'Now, *who* was it you wanted to ask about?'

'Jenny Bowles, sir. She has a place in the theatre there.'

'Ah now,' I said, wrinkling my brow. 'Is that the young person who's dresser to Miss Ackroyd?'

But how did he know she was there?

'That's right, sir. She and me are sweethearts.' Forebodings all confirmed! The boy looked at me with appeal in his face. 'She says as 'ow you're a very kind gentleman.'

I felt oddly gratified at that. I do seriously believe that, for all the humbug about 'free-born Englishmen', the humble in this country are as downtrodden as any in the world. I was not conscious of having done any particular acts of kindness to poor, dead Jenny, and I concluded that it was a general, inborn kindness she had seen in me. But then a thought struck me.

'It was good of her to say so. You have, er, communicated with her since she came to the theatre?'

'Just the once, sir.' He shuffled and looked down. 'I know she wasn't supposed to, and she wouldn't come out again because she said it was too dangerous. But we're courting, sir, and . . . well, it wasn't natural that we couldn't talk a little and – you know—'

'I see,' I said noncommittally. He drew his sleeve across his mouth and hurried on.

'We're both very poor, you see, sir, and hoping to be

married. We've dreamed of having a little shop, or an alehouse maybe.'

Oh, the dreams of the English to have their own little business, to do something-or-other in a small way and thus gain their independence! How it does ensnare and delude them, and how politicians lead them on in their delusion!

'I see. You're not a Londoner I can hear.'

'Oh no, sir. I'm an Essex man. Little village near Colchester. I'm hoping to take Jenny there when we're married, out of this nasty dirty 'ole. Young girls come to all sorts of harm in this city, as I'm sure you know, sir. But she'd found this way of getting a bit of money – something I don't rightly understand – and I'm afeared for her, sir. Folk like us get mixed up with the affairs of great folks at our peril.'

How sadly right he was.

'I'm sure you're fearing needlessly,' I said, sounding unconvincing even to myself.

'I don't think so, sir,' he said stubbornly. 'You see we had this system of signs.'

'Signs?'

'That's right, sir. Every night I waited here for it. I knew the window of the dressing-room she worked in, and every night she 'ung a dress in front of the window to show that she was all right. Then I could go home and sleep sound, sir.'

'I see . . . But you couldn't sleep sound last night?'

'I didn't sleep at all, sir. Never went 'ome.' Further forebodings jumped in my stomach, and probably showed in my face. I should never have left the enveloping darkness of Orange Street. The boy was intent on his explanations, and I hoped he hadn't noticed. 'I waited and waited and everything was later than usual because it was some kind of special performance, wasn't it, sir?'

'That's right: a first night.'

'Well, very late on you and some other gentlemen came out with some kind of stage stuff it looked like—'

My voice cracked as I said: 'Yes, a prop. It was needed at one of Mr Popper's other theatres.'

'I see, sir. It looked more like a trunk to me. But I don't

know much about theatres and the like. Never been to one, to tell you the truth. Not in my line. Well, then a bit later another gentleman came out and locked up the door – I think it would be Mr Popper, because I've seen him do that before – and he walked off a little unsteady-like. And that was all. There was no sign in the window all night.'

'But maybe she just forgot.'

He shook his head with the certainty of youth.

'Oh no, she wouldn't forget, sir. Not Jenny. Have you seen her today, sir?'

I gave the appearance of thinking.

'Er, no I haven't. But then I wouldn't in all probability, unless I went to Miss Ackroyd's dressing-room.'

'Did you see her yesterday, sir?'

Memories of that body in the poor stuff dress with the gash down the back rose uninvited. I repressed them.

'I can't recall that I did. Yesterday was very busy for me – it was one of my pieces that was being performed.'

'Did you hear anyone talk about her?'

'Not that I remember. Everyone was very excited by the performance, which went very well.'

'I see, sir,' he said, looking very crestfallen.

'Have you thought that Mr Popper could have given her a job in one of his other theatres? He has several, you know.'

That was true enough. Sweaty little flea-pits in parts of London no gentleman would visit or take his womenfolk to. The boy's face lit up.

'Is that so, sir?'

'Oh yes. If she had got herself involved in something . . . important, as you seem to think, she may have had to be moved for her own safety.'

God forgive me for a liar! The poor boy was heartened, and started to beseech me.

'Could you find out, sir? Could you find out where she's gone?'

'Well—'

'*Please*, sir. I must know she's all right.'

I was in a quandary what to do. The boy had to be staved off, without being given any definite – and certainly not any true – information about Jenny.

'I suppose I could find out *if* she's gone,' I said at last. 'I imagine they won't want it known *where* she's gone. After all, the reason she's been moved may be that they found out about you and her and decided that the Queen's was no longer safe enough.'

His face fell.

'Do you think so?'

'I really don't know. I know nothing about it.'

'But you'll find out, sir?'

'Well, I'll try. How do I get a message to you? Are you still working for Alderman Wood?'

'Yes, I am, sir. The wages in't too bad, him needing to think about his credit as an Alderman. The trouble with noble folk is they don't have to bother about their credit with anyone, and they pays according.'

'You could be right,' I said, in heartfelt tones.

'But I'd rather see you and talk,' the boy said, 'messages not being in my line. Will you be here tomorrow night?'

'Well, I'm not at the theatre. My piece is not playing. But I suppose I could come especially . . .'

I was very reluctant, but the boy drew his sleeve over his eyes.

'Please, sir. Please come.'

'Very well – er, I'm sorry: you haven't told me your name.'

'Davy, sir. Davy House.'

'Well, Davy, I'll see you tomorrow night.'

And I went on my way, leaving him to go back to Alderman Wood's or his lodging. I had rather liked the young man, liked his simple love, pitied him for the loss he as yet knew nothing about. But I regret for my own credit to say that as I walked home I was thinking mainly of how this new factor in the imbroglio could be turned to account with Lord Hertford and his steward.

CHAPTER TEN
Il Dissoluto Punito

I dressed myself with care for my encounter with Lord Hertford's steward and (I confidently expected) Lord Hertford himself. For such encounters I have a code of conduct which I have developed over the years: for example, it is obviously unwise to go too richly attired. What is less obvious is that it is unwise to dress too shabbily: if you look like a beggar you will be treated like a beggar and given ha'pence. A dignified middle course has to be steered: one should look and behave like the better class of tradesman – one who has supplied the best produce, given the best service, and now seeks adequate recompense for his pains. I was trained in such things by my dear father, God rest his soul, and I trust I have faithfully followed his precepts.

Blacks and browns, then, and a clean white stock. I took with me my ivory-handled cane, not because I need it (I have kept remarkably my young-man's figure and the vigour of my frame), but because it added to the dignified impression. I confess that as I made my way towards Manchester Square one or two of the acquaintances I met smiled, as if they could guess my errand from my clothes. At long last I reached the dignified pile that is Hertford House, and banged on the door. Lord Hertford's footman was supercilious in his manner, as all flunkies are to artists, but when I was shown into the steward's office it became clear that this was because the message had not yet filtered down to the lowest ranks. The steward's demeanour was quite different: cordial, frank, even respectful. It had never been so before, and it was clear he was under orders.

'Mr Mozart! I got your note. A slight chill in the air, is there not? Would you care for a glass of ratafia?'

I thought it would have been better if Lord Hertford had shown his appreciation of my services by putting in a token appearance himself. However, there was a silver tray on the steward's desk with decanter, glasses and a plate of delicious-looking biscuits. They looked inviting – I have a very sweet tooth. I bowed my acceptance, and we began the social business of sipping and nibbling as preliminaries to business. The steward, Mr de Fries, continued to be expansive and genial.

'His Lordship is most grateful to you for your help in that unfortunate little business,' he said. (Poor Jenny! – to be in death nothing but an unfortunate little business.) 'You were the right man in the right place at the right time.'

What precisely did that mean? That I was in luck in finding myself in a position to earn a substantial purse? Or that Lord Hertford had been in luck in having the best possible assistance to hand? I assumed the second interpretation.

'I certainly think it would have been unfortunate if His Lordship had been forced to rely on Mr Popper,' I murmured.

Mr de Fries nodded.

'Good point. Excellent point. A somewhat unreliable person, I believe?'

'Totally.'

'I will make the point to Lord Hertford. It is unfortunate that he is heavily committed to supporting Mr Popper's new opera season – a matter of three or four thousand pounds I believe.' He saw I was about to change my tune, so he held up his hand. 'But I think you may rely on him for the most forceful advocacy and all other support for your delightful operas.' He reached down into one of the desk's drawers. 'Meanwhile His Lordship hopes you will accept this as a small token of his appreciation.'

He handed over an exquisitely soft and substantial chamois bag. In it, my experienced hand told me, there

96

must be around eighty guineas. Adequate if not exactly generous. A man to whom generosity was second nature would surely have made it a hundred. I bowed my gratitude.

'His Lordship is too kind.'

Mr de Fries signified the end of our business.

'I will summon someone to escort you to your home or your banker's.'

Bankers! What use had I for bankers? Only people with money need bankers. His hand had gone towards the bell-rope, but I stayed it.

'Mr de Fries, I regret to say that something has come up – something of the utmost importance. I am afraid that I shall have to acquaint His Lordship with it personally.'

He looked displeased.

'Oh dear, are you sure that is necessary? Lord Hertford is *very* much occupied this morning.'

'I am sure he is. But I know that when His Lordship hears what I have to say he will understand why he had to hear of this new development in person.'

Mr de Fries hummed and ha-ed, then concluded that he would have to talk to His Lordship in person. I was left alone in his office for ten minutes (wasn't he afraid I'd pocket the silver ink-stand?), but then he came back, accompanied by Lord Hertford, who looked in no very good humour.

'Well, well, Mr Mozart, I hope this is of importance.'

I nodded confidently. Luckily I felt very sure of my ground (an infrequent state of mind for me when I am dealing with grand personages).

'It is, My Lord, and it can be shortly told. You remember Jenny Bowles mentioned that she had a sweetheart – a gardening boy at Alderman Wood's?'

'Yes.'

'He accosted me after the performance last night. He knew Jenny was concealed at the Queen's – they had met and talked since she went there. He saw us removing the body without understanding the significance of what he saw, and he is desperately anxious to know what has happened to Jenny.'

97

'Why should he assume anything has happened to the girl?'

'Because they had signs to each other, in the window. He knows she is no longer there.'

There was a silence lasting several seconds. The steward and his master looked at each other, then ahead in thought. At last Lord Hertford said:

'He must be dealt with.'

The blood rushed to my head, and I lost all the circumspection one must show in dealing with an English nobleman. I began spluttering in my outrage:

'My Lord, I couldn't possibly countenance . . . I am already in this much further than I would have wanted to be . . . The suggestion is outrageous . . . If anything were to happen to the young man I should be forced to. . .'

There was a second silence, almost as long as the first. Then Lord Hertford spoke with a silky suaveness.

'Mr Mozart, whatever do you imagine I was suggesting? That I was contemplating hiring ruffians to kill or incapacitate the young man? I assure you on the word of an English gentleman such a course never crossed my mind. My suggestion was and is that the young man be approached and his silence purchased.'

I was forced by the two rigid, disapproving faces before me to stammer apologies.

'My Lord, I do beg your pardon. I was too hasty, confused by all that has happened. But I do not believe the young man can be bought. Remember his sweetheart has been killed.'

'But not by us. Not by us.'

'Will he believe it?'

'He must believe it. It is clear the poor wench was killed by some enemy of the King who had at any price to prevent the Queen's degraded passions becoming public knowledge. Some Whig sympathiser it must have been.'

So that was to be the story. As a story it was perfectly plausible. But it was no use in the present crisis. I shook my head.

'My Lord, Whig and Tory mean nothing to such as Davy House. The people who cheer the Queen, the people who stoned this very house, are not Whigs, or radicals, or republicans. They cheer from human feeling, from a sort of deep down anger inside them – right or wrong – that a woman and a queen should be exposed as the Queen has been exposed. The political and constitutional subtleties are quite beyond them. All Davy House will understand is that you had his sweetheart concealed at the theatre for political reasons he cannot fathom, and that she was killed there. He will be grief-stricken and angry, and I would not trust too much to his *reason*.'

My long speech impressed My Lord and his steward. Lord Hertford unbent in his usual manner, and became almost genial.

'Let us sit down and discuss this. Another glass of ratafia, Mr Mozart? Put the biscuits beside him, Mr de Fries. They are delightful, are they not? Now, tell us precisely what the boy told you.'

I went through my talk with Davy in detail. Every word was etched on my mind. I told them not just everything of importance, but *everything*, and they listened intently. When I had finished Lord Hertford pondered.

'Let me make sure I entirely understand. The boy knew his sweetheart was at the Queen's, knew she was involved in something of moment. Did he know you were involved, Mr Mozart?'

I ground my teeth silently. How, why, *was* I involved?

'He gave no sign of it, My Lord.'

'Right. Now, he had talked to Jenny only once. He saw us on the night of Jenny's death. That was a damnable mistake. I should never have gone with you.' *He* should not have gone with *us*! 'Curse my coachman for a bungler!'

'He was looking for passers-by, My Lord,' I pointed out. 'Not for anyone concealed.'

'True enough. So the boy saw us, but did not understand what we were doing. And you have suggested that Jenny may be working at one of Mr Popper's other theatres?'

'It was all I could come up with on the spur of the moment.'

Lord Hertford shook his head. 'It was most resourceful. I shall not forget how much we owe you, still, in all this, Mr Mozart. Now, the question is, do you believe him? I mean generally.'

It was my turn to ponder.

'He has the ring of truth about him, My Lord,' I said finally.

'And yet . . . He claims that they met and talked only *once*. Does that seem natural? If Jenny – as she must have – had identified and used the key to the stage door, would she not have used it more than *once* if she knew that her lover was waiting outside?'

There is no doubting Lord Hertford's *brain*. Only his heart.

'It does seem likely, My Lord,' I admitted. 'But in what way is it material?'

'The more they talked the more the boy knew. On the other hand the more he can be shown to be a liar the easier it will be to bully him into silence. Is he still working at Alderman Woods?'

'Yes, he is. He says the pay is good.'

'Those damned radicals buy their popularity. So, he would not be easy to approach there. But you say you are meeting him again tonight?'

'That's right, My Lord. In the Haymarket.'

'Then we must use you, Mr Mozart. Tell him – let me see – tell him his young friend is indeed working at another theatre. And tell him he must come here and speak to Mr de Fries, who will supply him with all the details.'

'But what will he tell him, My Lord?'

'As little as possible. And he will attempt to buy his silence. That is not pretty, but it is the best we can do. The boy is poor, so he should be purchasable.' The feeling smote me that he could be talking about me. 'If he is exceptionally co-operative it might also mean that we have a spy in the Queen's camp.'

I refrained from pointing out that the usefulness of a gardener's boy as a spy would be limited. Lord Hertford now returned to his pressing business and Mr de Fries

100

summoned an under-footman to escort me to my banker's or to my house. He was a dour young man, and I did not bother to explain to him that people who live from day to day have no use for bankers. He put the hefty chamois bundle into a battered leather bag and we walked in the direction of Covent Garden. I had enough to think about without making conversation. As we neared my apartment I decided to make a brief detour in the direction of the Strand and Mr Benbow's Chop House. That gentleman was just bustling up to refuse me further credit when I gestured towards his back room. That was where long-standing bills were settled, or reduced. There the under-footman opened the homely bag, I rummaged in the more luxurious one and handed to Mr Benbow five golden guineas. It was a satisfying moment, and would have been still more so if Mr Benbow's face had expressed gratification instead of surprise. Then we went on to Henrietta Street and I dismissed the man with a florin which I had taken with me for that purpose. Then, having extracted three guineas for my immediate use I locked the bag away in the top of the closet I usually use for any substantial windfalls.

What I was to do next I had thought about on the walk home, but I nevertheless poured myself a glass of Madeira and thought it over again. Even on further consideration it seemed the right thing to do. I went to my desk, made space amid the multifarious piles of music paper, and wrote the following in clear capitals:

TO DAVY HOUSE:
DANGER. DO NOT COME TO HAYMARKET TONIGHT. SUGGEST YOU EITHER STAY WITHIN ALDERMAN WOOD'S HOUSE AND GROUNDS OR DISAPPEAR TO SOMEWHERE WHERE YOU ARE NOT KNOWN FOR THE NEXT WEEK OR TWO.

W.G. MOZART

It read very melodramatically I know, but it had to be put simply for Davy's comprehension. Simplification is the essence of melodrama. I went in search of Jo, my bright

101

urchin in the Strand, impressed the message on him verbally in case Davy could not read at all (as my urchin assuredly could not), then expended another florin to impress upon him the importance of getting the message to Davy. Knowing my usual scale of rewards the urchin first looked at me as if I had gone as mad as the late King, then hallooed with delight and sped off as if he had the heels of Mercury.

How to fill the hours until night? I was too disturbed in my mind to return to my Wind Serenade or to put the finishing touches to the last act of *Le Comari di Windsor*. I first wrote to Lady Hertford at Royal Lodge, Windsor Castle, detailing the amount which, according to Mr de Fries, her Lord had so far committed to the opera season. I am not proud of the letter, which was both disloyal and against my own greater interests, so I shall not reproduce it. To get the taste out of my mouth I went to dine at Mallory's in Holborn, where the game is peerless. A brace of pheasants and a pint of claret put me in much better humour, and it was pleasant once in a way to pay in coin of the realm. There was still time to be filled in before I went to meet – or rather, as I hoped, *not* to meet – Davy House.

There was an unusually large crowd outside Covent Garden as I returned home. Their audiences are usually gratifyingly meagre because their prices are high and their standards low. Looking at the placards I saw that the piece to be played was Boieldieu's *Jean de Paris*, which the transcendent genius of Mr Bishop had adapted to English taste. Not a new piece or a particularly popular one. I frowned in mystification.

'They say the King is coming,' said a man beside me, seeing my puzzlement. 'That's what they're waiting to see.'

I nodded, and probably gained the reputation with him of a toady by immediately going in and paying for a good seat. I did not have long to wait for the entertainment to start. First of all noises penetrated to the Circle that were not the sounds of cheering. Five minutes later the door to the royal box was opened by the tallest flunkies in the house and Prinny walked in at a stately pace. The house seemed to erupt in a chorus of boos and catcalls, through

102

which could be discerned various jeering sobriquets.

'Mr Hertford.'

'Mr Conyngham.'

'Mr Fitzherbert.'

The vilification came mainly from the cheaper seats, but some boos came from all parts of the theatre. Prinny was horribly discomposed. I was reminded of 'The Rake Punished', the other title of my *Don Giovanni* (on which subject my Lord Byron is presently publishing a disgraceful poem which I decline to read). As the members of the royal party filed, disconcerted, into the box some of the people in the better parts of the house began applauding the King with simulated enthusiasm. I myself joined in, and the King regained some of that sunny grace and equanimity which he displayed in private. He bowed to the applauding parts of the house with an air which seemed to single out each one of us, including myself, for dignified royal acknowledgement. Our actions, of course, stimulated the barrackers, and they brought out new nicknames for him, including 'Fatty' and 'The Prince of Whales'. You do not need to be clever or original to wound. It was many minutes (and Mr Bishop had long been in front of his players with his silly conducting stick) before the house subsided into something like silence.

I stuck two acts of the piece. If I must listen to mellifluous twaddle I would prefer it to be my own. I can do no better in characterising Boieldieu's piece than say that I couldn't tell where his music ended and young (or youngish) Bishop's began. But before I left the theatre I saw something that intrigued and surprised me. I am not one of those who gape at royal personages, and once the piece started I averted my eyes from the royal box. However as the party filed back at the end of the first intermission I thought I discerned a face I knew. Seated among the less important (because untitled) personages at the back of the box was – surely my eyes did not deceive me? – the divine Therese Hubermann-Cortino and her gorilla of a husband.

Thought and speculation about the significance of her presence there occupied my mind satisfactorily during the second helping of musical gruel. Shortly after I left the theatre and was walking through Seven Dials I realised that the King had taken the same decision as I had: derisory catcalls from the direction of Covent Garden told me he was leaving the theatre.

I had half a pint of Amontillado in a Soho tavern notable, even among such establishments, for its dirt and the rudeness of its keeper. Then I repaired to the Haymarket and walked up and down for an hour and more waiting for Davy House who did not (I was pleased and relieved to find) turn up. I had a distinct impression, though, that someone else was there, and watching me. A spy from Lord Hertford, I had no doubt, set on by him or his steward to make sure I did what I had been told to do.

Then I went to home and bed, where I dreamed of a splendid Mass in C Minor. I always dream music, but I can seldom write any of it down when I wake up. On the morrow I wrote to Lord Hertford to acquaint him (unnecessarily, I was quite sure) with the fact that Davy had not turned up. Two hours later I received a note ordering me (or rather asking me in an aristocratic kind of way) to wait for him again that night, and if he did not appear bidding me to a conference at Hertford House the day after. My involvement with my betters was not over. How I wished it were!

CHAPTER ELEVEN
I'll Play the Tune

And so I spent another hour or two the next night, after the third performance of *A Call to Arms*, pacing up and down the Haymarket, cursing in my mind my involvement with Lord Hertford and his schemes. It wasn't as though he was even particularly generous, considering the legal danger he was getting me into. Someone like Lord Egremere would have been much more open-handed – Whig peers usually are, probably because they have been out of office for so long that they have to be.

The thought of Lord Egremere brought back to my mind the question of who had killed poor Jenny Bowles. If that was a political crime then it must have been done by a Whig or a radical, an opponent of the King who knew what Jenny had overheard but didn't know of the plan to have a substitute Jenny appear before the Lords. There must have been any number of Whigs and radicals in the audience that evening. Members of the audience do quite frequently penetrate backstage: the morals of singers and actors are not, alas, of the most spotless. Members of the aristocracy and the royal family are particularly attracted by the freedoms of theatre people. But I had to remember that any member of the Queen's troupe, actor, singer, musician or menial, could be an opponent of the King. Probably most of them were. And any of them who wasn't could probably have been bought – though perhaps few could have been bought to commit such a deed as a killing. The question one kept coming back to was: who knew about Jenny? It was a question that could have dreadful implications for Betty Ackroyd, if the charade before the House of Lords was persisted in.

Anyway, the next day a conference assembled in a small sitting-room on the first floor of Hertford House. We made an ill-assorted group in all that rather stuffy grandeur. There was Mr Popper shuffling uneasily and looking as if he wished he were a thousand miles away. An opera manager would not normally see the living quarters of a great house. At best he would be granted an interview in the offices. Then there was Betty Ackroyd, much more confident and at home, or pretending to be, myself, Mr de Fries, and finally Lord Hertford himself. Coffee was served, and then the footman and maid were ordered to withdraw. People surrounded by armies of servants are people surrounded by armies of spies.

'So here we are,' said Lord Hertford. 'All those who knew of poor Jenny Bowles and her story.'

I looked straight ahead of me, and I imagine Betty Ackroyd did the same. We both knew of at least one more person who knew: Bradley Hartshead. I went over in my own mind other possibles who knew: Davy House perhaps had some dim inkling, perhaps something more concrete. Lady Hertford? The King? The Prime Minister? Surely Lord Hertford had not decided on his plan without consultation with anyone more important than his own steward? I felt sure in my mind that the King had been told: I believed the whole thing (whether Jenny's story was true or not) was a plan to regain the favour of the King and the influence the Hertfords had formerly had with him – influence which was slipping away as Lady Hertford was being replaced as principal mistress by Lady Conyngham. It was a cold plot designed to keep the spoils of office, the office being the age-old one of first whore.

'Now,' said Lord Hertford, 'let's get down to business. On the surface of things the death of Bowles does not make any difference to our plans.' He cleared his throat, looked at me, then looked at Mr Popper. 'This will be news to some of you, but we had already decided that putting Bowles in front of the assembled House of Lords was simply not feasible. Miss Ackroyd is a brilliant mimic, and

106

we were planning that she should impersonate her before the House of Lords, so that her story could be properly told.'

He looked around again, and I put on the expected expression of surprise.

'Brilliant, My Lord,' I said.

'A cunning notion, I thought,' he said with a cold little smile of self-congratulation. 'I have no doubt it would have been successful. And it still may be. Miss Ackroyd could go, give her testimony, be spirited away afterwards and – and then disappear.'

We all went through the motions of thinking this over.

'Would her – my – disappearance not lessen the value of the testimony?' asked Betty Ackroyd.

'I think not. With the passions of the mob at the pitch they are now, Jenny herself would have had to be whisked away and hidden. No, if the testimony is made before the Lords it will have a stunning effect. It will destroy the Queen's case.'

He was a great deal too complacent. I had no doubt that he was leading us – and particularly Betty – into dangers we had hardly grasped. I had no doubt, either, that he would not be in there sharing the dangers with us. Aristocrats and politicians never are. I had to demolish the plan, but I had to proceed with the utmost cunning. I have to admit I am rather good (I have had to be) at the art of scheming. I may occasionally be wrong about people, but in the art of plotting to get my own way I have few equals. In this case it was not my own pecuniary advantage that was the goal in view, but the safety of Betty Ackroyd.

'Are the dangers not greater now?' I asked respectfully.

'I do not see that they are,' said Lord Hertford, his brow furrowed. 'Why so?'

'Because there has been a death,' I said. 'Before if Miss Ackroyd's impersonation was found out, Jenny Bowles could have been produced. Whether her story would have been believed after the imposture is another matter, but she could have been produced. Now she cannot, and if the imposture is discovered then questions are going to be asked as to what has happened to her.'

Lord Hertford hummed and hawed. Finally, after some thought, he raised his head.

'That is true, but I do not think it is conclusive against the scheme. There is no reaason to believe the impersonation will be discovered. Who could discover it? That would demand that a member of Alderman Wood's staff actually be at the trial. That is unthinkable, with the press of persons of rank for seats. Secondly, if a kitchen-maid goes missing who is to be surprised or suspicious at that?' He looked at Mr de Fries. 'Surely domestic staff move on, get new places, find themselves in an interesting condition or whatever, all the time?'

'Particularly the lower servants,' murmured the steward.

'Exactly. So if we are unable to produce Jenny we simply say we found her a position in one of Mr Popper's other theatres – where shall we say?—'

'Deptford, perhaps,' suggested that artistic luminary. 'A lot of rough types in Deptford.'

'Brilliant suggestion,' said his lordship perfunctorily. 'And we say she simply disappeared, probably took up with some seaman or other, and that should be the end of the matter. No, Mr Mozart, my feeling is that, as soon as the Queen's Defence have produced their last witness, which will probably be Tuesday or Wednesday of next week, we should immediately summon our additional witness – Miss Ackroyd here, doing her very remarkable impersonation of Jenny Bowles.'

There seemed to be in the room the silence of consent. There very often is, when an aristocrat has spoken.

'Would you permit me, My Lord, to act as *advocatus diaboli* in this matter?' I asked, conscious I was risking the loss of his favour, but knowing that something had to be done to counter his cavalier dismissal of danger to anyone except himself. 'A thankless position but a useful one when one is considering a course of action.'

'By all means, Mr Mozart,' said Lord Hertford, impeccably courteous.

'I think we are forgetting one or two things. First there is Jenny's sweetheart, Davy House. The boy is naturally concerned about her, but I believe he is unsuspicious –

unsuspicious about her actual fate, that is. That is only my judgment, since of course only I have talked to him. On the other hand the boy failed to keep his appointment with me.'

'What are you suggesting?' asked Lord Hertford, with a touch of steel in his voice. He had not forgotten, clearly, my assumption that he would like to have him murdered.

'I am suggesting nothing, My Lord, merely considering possibilities. And one possibility is that, even if he is unsuspicious himself, he has confided his worries about Jenny to someone higher than himself in Alderman Wood's household. Perhaps even to the Alderman himself.'

'That rascal!'

I bowed my agreement. Certainly Alderman Wood was a rascal, but I was not at all sure that Lord Hertford was not, in his more refined way, his equal in rascality. Only of course one suppresses such thoughts about a brother Mason.

'A rascal with a keen brain, My Lord, and a vast deal of cunning. Let us put Davy's knowledge at its lowest; let us say that he went along to Alderman Wood, or to someone close to him, with the story that his sweetheart had overheard something detrimental to the Queen and her interests—'

'Do we know that he knows that?'

'No, My Lord. But we don't *know* that he doesn't. Let's conjecture that he knows Jenny's story, that he tells Alderman Wood that she took it to you, My Lord, and was then concealed at the Queen's Theatre. The Alderman hardly needs to put two and two together to decide that you intended making good use of Jenny's revelations.'

'Hmmm . . .' said Lord Hertford. 'You make a good devil's advocate, Mr Mozart. You missed your vocation.'

'I hope *not*, My Lord. Now say Davy, pressed to tell all he knows, goes on to narrate the scene he witnessed close to midnight in the Haymarket with you, me and the box. Davy himself is rustic, unsuspicious. The Alderman and his associates are neither of these things. They might well conjecture a death and the concealment of that death.

This would no doubt confuse them. Frankly it confuses us, does it not? But what a weapon their mere suspicion gives them!'

There was a lot of uneasy shifting in chairs at this (helped by the fact that the chairs, like so many in stately surroundings, were not very comfortable). Even Betty now seemed to realise that, like most of us, she was further into dubious transactions than was good for her. We all knew that we were so because of Lord Hertford. And we all suspected that, should things go wrong, it would not be he who shouldered the blame.

'You give us pause for thought,' admitted Mr de Fries.

'One point more – my last,' I went on. 'You said, My Lord, that all those who knew of Jenny Bowles and her story are in this room.' I purposely did not look at Betty Ackroyd. I had no intention of revealing Bradley Hartshead's knowledge of the substitution plot. 'But is this so? I fear I shall have to be particular, My Lord. Does Lady Hertford know?'

'Well, yes, she—'

'Does the King now?'

'Oh, but of course inevitably he—'

'I yield to no one in my admiration for the King's charm, courtesy and exquisite taste,' I said, excepting in my mind his rotten taste in operatic composers, 'but one of the qualities he is not known for is discretion. We must speak bluntly, My Lord, or this matter will not have been considered thoroughly.'

'Of course, of course.'

'Has the Prime Minister been told? Any member of his government? The law officers?'

'That I really can't say.'

'Then I come back to the fact that we cannot ignore about Jenny: someone knew about her and her story, because someone killed her. If we try to say knowledge of her was confined to the people in this room, we are almost saying one of us killed her. And I do not for one moment think that was the case.'

'No, no, of course not. That's unthinkable. Goes without saying . . .' Lord Hertford remained for a minute or two in

110

a profound reverie. Even when he spoke he clearly had not come to any conclusion. 'I have put someone on to pumping Alderman Wood's servants in their off-duty time. They say that the boy Davy House is no longer there. That proves nothing, of course.'

'Nothing at all,' I agreed. 'You spirited Jenny away as soon as you heard her tale. They may have done the same, and they may be preparing to spring him on us, as we were preparing to spring her on them.'

These 'we's were used with great reluctance, but it seemed politic to associate myself with My Lord and his party, since I had so much to gain from him. Still, I wished I'd been given a choice . . .

Lord Hertford shook his head in frustration.

'It goes against the grain. We had the crowning piece in the King's case against the Princess. We still have it – we *know* of her appalling and degrading tastes and habits. And yet it seems that we can't use it.'

'Could you not use the information in another way?' suggested Mr Popper timidly. 'Set people to spread rumours . . .'

'My dear sir, rumours about the Queen's conduct are legion. Every day brings fresh ones. What we had was *evidence.*'

'There is the possibility of finding the watermen concerned,' said Mr de Fries, without great conviction. 'There is no guarantee that they would be willing to give testimony, but we are making efforts in that direction.'

'Wouldn't *any* waterman do?' asked Betty Ackroyd. 'Surely most of them would lie for a consideration – as apparently they were willing to lie with her for one?'

There was a small titter at this. It was Mr Popper. Lord Hertford looked disapproving.

'Yes, they would lie,' he said. 'Everyone knows that. That's why I am not hopeful, even if we found the ones who serviced the Queen, that their evidence would be believed.'

Depression hung over the room like the smoke on a Northern factory town. Lord Hertford's exasperation and frustration were almost palpable. We all sat watching him, uncertain. Finally he rose in a gesture of dismissal.

111

'We seem hemmed in at every turn. We cannot make a decision here today. Leave it with me, gentlemen, Miss Ackroyd. I am grateful to you for your time . . .'

Mr de Fries summoned a footman from the uncompanionable vastnesses of Hertford House, and we were ushered down that splendid staircase and out into Manchester Square. I was thoughtful. I had by implication lied about Davy House, since I knew perfectly well why he had disappeared. That was something for my next visit to the Confessional. Again I had been unusually vocal and unusually forceful during the meeting, and it looked as if my arguments would be influential in a decision to abandon the plan. It seems to me now that that is one of the most satisfactory aspects to my involvement in the sorry business. Then I was more dubious, and hoped it would not lead to Lord Hertford feeling less obliged to me – in particular interesting himself less in the performance of my operas.

Betty Ackroyd noticed my thoughtfulness and came up behind me as we began the long walk to the Haymarket.

'You spoke very well, Mr Mozart.'

'Thank you, my dear.'

'You were obviously eager to see the plan abandoned.'

'I was, I was.'

'Why? Was it chivalry towards the Queen?'

I shook my head.

'Hardly. Or only to a very small degree. I fear the lady herself somewhat repels the whole notion of chivalry . . . No, my main concern was that you should not ruin the wonderful career that awaits you even before it has begun.'

I was surprised that she bridled somewhat at that.

'Would it not have been courtesy, Mr Mozart, to consult me, who am most concerned in the matter, before you ruined my chance in this way? A woman does not get many such chances.' She looked up at me with an expression that was almost hostile. Oh dear! Surely Betty Ackroyd was not going to prove one of these 'burden of womanhood' girls – another Mary Woolston-whatever-it-was? But she added a complaint that was more practical than theoretical. 'I had been promised a very substantial gift by Lord Hertford.'

I looked at her pityingly.

112

'My dear, you cannot base your life on gifts from noblemen. There is more to be made from a career as a great singer than is ever likely to be wrung from such as Lord Hertford.'

'Oh? And 'ave you made so much from a career in the theatre that you can spurn gifts from the nobs?' she asked, with a strong touch of Bradford back in her voice. I could have told her that prima donnas made infinitely more than mere composers, but her mood suddenly changed. 'But let's not quarrel, Mr Mozart. You didn't tell about Bradley, and I'm grateful to you for that. If you had, the fat would really have been in the fire!'

I would have liked to ask her why. I felt a great deal of curiosity – or different curiosities – about her origins and private life, but I was prevented by feelings of delicacy from straying into that territory. Instead I said:

'On the day Jenny died I seem to remember she'd failed to do something – was it iron your second act costume?'

'Yes. I was very annoyed. Awful to think of now.'

'But she was there in the dressing-room at interval time?'

'Oh yes – that's why it's awful to think of now. I wish I had been nicer to her.'

'Was she pretty much as usual?'

Betty shook her head.

'No, not exactly. Usually she was sort of inert, just went on doing things without any emotion. That night she was flurried, red-faced, and I thought she'd been crying.'

'As if something had happened during the first act?'

Betty grimaced.

'Yes, I suppose so. That does seem likely. I just didn't think at the time, and I snapped at her. She'd been happier before that, at the thought of not having to give evidence. Then she started going weepy again. Of course I should have asked her what was the matter, but things were getting exciting in the theatre and ... well, I just didn't. I regret it now.'

'Did she normally come to the wings, for if she was needed?'

'If she *was* needed for a costume change she did, but she

113

wasn't for *A Call to Arms*. She may have been there at some stage, but I can't recall seeing her. The theatre was a great mystery to Jenny – some kind of secular ritual she despaired of penetrating. I don't think she'd quite fathomed that we were different people in the play to ourselves off stage.' She was silent for a moment, then she threw a look in my direction. 'I'm not thinking about her death. There's nothing I can do now, and I think it's . . . safer.'

It was a clear warning, or at least a piece of advice. I thought over both the warning and the information she'd given me during the rest of our walk to the Queen's Theatre. That night we were performing *Arthur and Antoinette*, an old piece set at the time of the French Revolution. It was already a dated piece, now that the pendulum has swung back towards the old regimes and conservative ways. Odd that people think it is back there permanently, forgetting it is in the nature of pendula to swing. The riots in favour of the Queen will have reminded the wise of this. Anyway the piece is full of noble-minded aristocrats and villainous French townsmen. The Antoinette of the title is not the sweet, tragic Austrian princess for whom and with whom I played in my childhood but a sugar-stick of an aristocrat in peril of decapitation on the guillotine, rescued by the impeccably tedious English hero Arthur. I had only decided to direct the piece from the fortepiano in order to talk to people about events on the evening of the first night of *A Call to Arms*. It must be said I got nothing of value. Actors remember who upstaged them, who ruined their best lines or made them miss a top note, but otherwise of things connected with other people they are largely unconscious.

After the performance, played to a lethargic audience of shopkeepers and bank clerks, I walked home as usual. The nights were getting chilly (*chillier*, I should say – they are always chilly in this god-forsaken country). As I negotiated the usual perils of drunkards, whores, beggars, and people sleeping in doorways and huddled in crates I pondered my day's work. I really had been rather cunning. The scheming that I had undertaken in the course of my life

114

had mostly been connected (of absolute necessity) with financial matters, but that day I had used my cunning for higher ends: I prided myself that I had effectively scuppered Lord Hertford's plan to involve Betty still further in his plot. I promised myself that as soon as I found out that this was indeed so, I would reward myself with a visit to my dear son Charles Thomas in Wakefield. My family are very dear to me and all doing very respectably (though of course lacking the *honoured* places in Society that would be theirs as the children of a great composer in dear, dear Austria).

I reached Henrietta Street and opened the outside door, shutting and locking it against the city's vagabonds. I walked up the stairs to my apartment and was just inserting the key in the door when I was startled by a form emerging from the gloom of the landing behind me. I swung round and was confronted by a stocky shape.

'Mr Mozart, will you let me come in? I'm frightened and I don't know what to do.'

It was the voice of Davy House.

CHAPTER TWELVE
Mann und Weib, und Weib und Mann

I pulled Davy into my apartment, then closed and locked the door. I went round as calmly as I could lighting candles and lamps, but thinking furiously the while. I had to consider not just his situation, but my own. Then I looked at him, standing uncertainly by the door, his hands still shaking.

'Come and sit down,' I said. 'You look exhausted.'

He looked nervously round the room, as if afraid to come away from the door.

'I live alone,' I said. 'There's no one else here. Come along, and I'll give you something to warm you up.'

He came further into the room, still hesitant, and I gestured towards my comfortable old sofa. He sat nervously on the edge of it. I went and poured a glass of my second-best cognac.

'Drink this,' I said. 'It will do you good.' He drained the glass, then coughed and spluttered, drawing his sleeve over his mouth. 'Feel better now?'

He nodded.

'That's powerful stuff.'

'Powerful and good for you,' I said, taking a glass. 'What's made you so frightened?'

'Your note. And other things.'

'I see,' I said, trying to keep my voice low and calm. 'My note wasn't meant to frighten you, just to make you more careful. I wanted to put you on your guard. I thought that if you stayed within Alderman Wood's house grounds—'

116

'I don't live at Alderman Wood's house,' said Davy, looking up at me. 'I'm just one of the gardening boys. I got a bed at Old Simon Mullins's house in Dover Street.'

'I see. So you had to go back and forth.'

'Aye.' He hesitated. 'And anyway it wasn't comfortable for me at Alderman Wood's any more.'

'Oh. Why?'

'They'd begun to talk. At first when Jenny disappeared they didn't reckon nothing to it – just thought she'd found a new boyfriend and gone off with him. But then these rumours started going round—'

Still keeping my voice level and unfrightening I asked: 'Rumours? What exactly were the rumours?'

'Wasn't no "exactly" to them. All kinds of rumours. But what they come down to seemed to be that the Queen's enemies had something up their sleeves. And people seemed to be saying it had something to do with goings-on while she was staying at our house. Hers – the Queen's goings-on. And then they connected up with Jenny suddenly going missing, there was talk in the servants' hall which must have been taken above stairs, and they started looking at me curious-like, and then asking questions.'

'What did you tell them?'

'Nothing. I didn't know nothing, hardly. But I said we'd quarrelled and she must have found another sweetheart.' He looked miserably down at his rough hands. 'That wasn't true. We never quarrelled, Jenny and me. But I wanted to stop them looking at me like *I'd* done something.'

'But by then you knew where Jenny was?'

'Oh aye. But I wasn't going to give her away, was I?'

'I'm sure you wouldn't.'

He leaned forward, struggling to explain the course of events.

'She'd sent me a note, written by one of the footmen at the theatre. I puzzled it out. So we met that time, and we had this arrangement with signs like I told you about . . . Then suddenly it seemed like she wasn't there any longer, and then I spoke to you and got your note. I tell you, I was frightened, Mr Mozart. It was like Jenny and me had got

117

ourselves mixed up wi' things we didn't ought to know nothing about.'

'I think that *is* the long and the short of it,' I said sadly. 'The affairs of the great ones.'

'So I felt, somehow, as though I couldn't trust the people at Alderman Wood's, and I couldn't trust still less the people Jenny had gone to. So I just took off, like Jenny did, without giving my notice or anything. Only she had somewhere to go, and I got nowhere. I just been tramping the streets, and the further I go from the West End the safer I feel, but that's not right, because the West End's where Jenny is, leastways where she *was*. So I come back, and then I feel everyone's watching me, or at any road *looking* for me. You feel eyes scanning you, following your back, and you get scared again.'

His voice faded into silence. I took his glass and poured another measure of brandy, pouring one for myself at the same time.

'Have this. Drink it more slowly this time.'

He sipped, then looked up at me.

'Mr Mozart, what's going on?'

I had already taken my decision on what to tell him. I sat down beside him.

'Davy, I'm afraid I've got very bad news for you. Jenny is dead.'

He looked at me for a moment, stunned. Then his face crumpled like a paper bag and he bent forward, his shoulders racked with sobbing. I took his glass from his hand, and let him cry for a minute or two. Then I raised him and made him drink a little more. His honest face was red and blotchy. Once again he drew his sleeve over his face, this time to wipe his eyes.

'How did it happen, Mr Mozart? How did my Jenny die?'

'I think, Davy, she got involved in matters that were far more dangerous than she understood.'

I gave him a very simplified version of the events leading up to Jenny's death. I said she'd overheard things that told her that the Queen had behaved in a wicked and immoral way when she was staying at Alderman Wood's house. I said she had taken her knowledge to friends of the King, who had hidden her at the Queen's Theatre. Then knowledge of her whereabouts and her story had somehow got out, and someone had killed her to prevent her giving her evidence against the Queen. To avoid any scandal her death was then hushed up.

Davy took in this tendentious account with a puzzled frown on his tear-stained face.

'But where do I come in? Am I still in danger?'

'I fear so, Davy. I fear people suspect that you know too much. Maybe people on *both* sides.'

'But I don't know nothing! . . . What am I to do?'

I took a sudden decision.

'You must stay here.'

'Here?' he gazed around the dimly-lit apartment. 'Oh, I couldn't stay here, Mr Mozart. It's much too grand. I never slept anywhere like this before.'

It was the first time my humble and none-too-clean abode had been called grand. I smiled.

'It's not grand at all, Davy. There's a small bedroom that is very seldom used, and you can sleep there. You'll feel quite at home. I am going North for two or three weeks, to visit my son. Everyone at the Theatre will know that I am away so nobody will come here. If anybody else calls, *don't answer the door*. Don't even shout from inside. My little maid can keep coming in, and will buy whatever food and drink you need. I'll leave some money with her—'

'I don't need money, Mr Mozart. I've got plenty.' He produced from his pockets a couple of shillings and some pence. 'It's not money that bothers me, it's knowing where I'll be safe. Though with Jenny gone . . .'

'With Jenny gone you've still got your life ahead of you – and a good life it will be. You'll be safe here, if you're sensible. I'm not sure what we should tell Ann. She's not very bright, so she'll accept anything we tell her. Can you sing?'

'Sing? A little bit. I used to be in the church choir.'

He launched into 'The Jolly Ploughboy', a loathsomely insistent little jingle. I held up my hand.

'That will do. It's a nice enough voice. We'll tell her I'm

119

training you to be a singer, but I'll be called away to my son's. And while I'm away you will not need to go out. It will be a tedious time for you, but you will be safe.'

So that was how things were arranged. I told them at the theatre that I would be going into Yorkshire for a short visit. I was busy there most evenings, to ensure that the various pieces in the repertoire were sprucely played and sung, thus preparing the company for my absence and earning myself a modicum of money for the trip (paid by Mr Popper with the usual managerial reluctance). During these busy days I was told by Betty Ackroyd that the idea of bringing before the House of Lords evidence of the Queen's infamy (her word, said with a grin) had been given up. I was delighted. My advocacy of caution had born fruit.

However this news did not change my plans for Davy. Many people on both sides might still believe that he knew too much. The poor and powerless of this world are all too often held to be dispensable by the great ones, and it would be easy to hire a pack of ruffians to make sure he was never heard of again. England, these days, is almost Italian in the prevalence of bravos prepared to kill for money. Many of us fear that law and order are breaking down entirely. Davy meanwhile made himself useful in my apartment, repairing and renovating, he being quite a considerable handyman. He could also cook a simple meal, and persuaded me to show him how to wait at table. It was a pleasure having him there, he was so biddable and teachable.

Five days after his dramatic coming I took the coach to Leeds. I will not bore you with the details of the uncomfortable and tedious journey – the unspeakable state of the roads, the dirty inns, the terrible boredom of travelling through wet, flat Lincolnshire, especially to one who was born the child of mountains and valleys. Suffice to say that when, on the evening of the second day, I arrived at Wakefield, Charles Thomas and his little family were delighted to see me, and showered me with love and Northern hospitality.

The next few days were devoted to family and to music.

Many excellent practitioners of my art wished to pay their respects, and I was taken to hear some of the truly excellent choirs which abound in the North. All the choirmasters and choristers were united in praising my arrangement of the *Messiah* (damn Handel!) which they all used every year, at no cost to themselves and with no benefit to me. I paid a visit with Charles Thomas to Miss Mangnall's school, where I talked as much as possible to the little girls and as little as possible to the formidable preceptress who owned and administered the place. I whiled away the time while my son was engaged in his teaching duties by talking to a sweet but sickly-looking family from over Keighley way, who were inspecting the school for their eldest daughters.

I had asked my son when writing to advise him of my visit if he could procure for me written permission to see over Lady Hertford's magnificent property of Temple Newsam, near neighbouring Leeds. I would not have done so if I thought the lady herself would be there, but I knew she would not, and it seemed an opportunity to learn more of her and her husband in their capacity not as luminaries of the Court but as Northern squires, or rather grandees. My son is a friend of the Bishop of Wakefield, who put a coach and horses at my disposal, and so, some five days after my arrival, I drew up in the magnificent courtyard of the House in a style more dignified than I could have expected.

It was a pleasant autumn day, and I stood in the sunlight admiring first the splendid rolling grounds of the parkland around, then the warm, approachable building. Clearly Lady Hertford was a woman of great substance in this county – but that I knew already. As I haltingly made out the pious and patriotic inscription worked into the balustrade around the house I reflected that honour and allegiance to the King and loving affection among his subjects were no easier under George IV than they had been under Charles I, very different though the two monarchs were.

The comfortable but sharp-eyed housekeeper was welcoming, and regretted that, such was the press of visitors, the butler was engaged with another party. She asked if I would be content to be shown around by Thomas the footman. I expressed myself more than happy with Thomas.

Even before we had finished inspecting the Great Hall I had gained an impression that Thomas was discontented. As we passed through to visit the smaller rooms on the ground floor I began to engage him in conversation.

'Are Lord and Lady Hertford frequently in residence?' I asked.

'Generally once a year, sir,' he muttered. 'Though not next year.'

'Not next year?'

'The Coronation, so 'tis said.' Here was a pause during which he seemed to be sizing me up. His next words came out with the force of a new grievance coming on top of many earlier ones. 'They're laying people off, because they won't be coming up, and because of the expense of the Coronation.'

'Ah,' I said. 'And you are one of them.'

'Aye, I am that. These are rotten hard times, but they don't take no account of that.'

I left a sympathetic pause, and then said:

'Your mistress does not have the reputation of an open-handed lady.'

He lowered his voice to a near-whisper.

'She's a damned screw! If I had my way I'd never work for the gentry again, but I've nothing saved up. No chance of saving when you work for *her*!'

'You don't surprise me. I have occasionally encountered the lady in the theatre, and at Court.'

'Ha! She's no better than she should be, for all her airs. A woman of her age too!'

'The King seems to prefer ladies of a certain ... maturity.'

'With wine there's a time of maturity and there's a time when it starts to go off. I'd have thought she was well into the going-off period.'

Stinginess does not breed loyalty.

'My Lord seems a very ... tolerant husband.'

'He certainly seems to take to the horns as to the manner born,' he said, putting me in mind of Master Ford in my new opera, though Lord Hertford was certainly not a madly jealous cuckold. 'But it's different with great folk when they marry, isn't it?' the footman went on.

'Is it?'

'Seems so,' he said, becoming positively expansive. 'I mean if a working chap like me marries, his wife expects him to be faithful to her. If Warren – that's Cook's husband – so much as looks at one of the maids he gets a warning. If Mrs Warren thought anything had really been going on – well! There *would* be an explosion, I can tell you.'

'Yes, I suppose it's *not* like that with the aristocracy.'

'O' course it's not. I suppose it's because they marry to get heirs, to "ensure the line", as Mr Warren puts it. They say Lady Hertford was a pretty little thing when she was a girl – hard to imagine now. He was a lot older, and he'd been married before, I think. They had several children, and there was one son to make sure the nation would never want for a Marquis of Hertford – not that I've ever personally felt the want – and then they pretty much went their own ways.'

'Oh yes?'

He nodded sagely.

'Have done for years now. The marriage is pretty much of a business partnership.'

'But they stay together.'

'Oh yes. Even sleep together on occasion. But he's had women all over the place around here.'

This was new. This was interesting.

'Oh really? They're well known, are they?'

'Oh yes, everyone knows who they are. You might say they're women of consequence – *as* a consequence of his favours. Not that he loads them with money or expensive presents. That's not at all My Lord's way, as you seem to have found yourself, sir. But he makes sure they've got a respectable living. Wouldn't suit his ideas of his own dignity otherwise.'

'I see,' I said. We started up the old wooden staircase,

and I said no more, for fear of being overheard. It was only when we came into the magnificent Long Gallery, and found ourselves alone there, that I resumed the conversation.

'Who were the principal of His Lordship's . . . er, lady friends?'

He grinned.

'No question about that. You can go and see her if you've a mind.'

'Really?'

'She's landlady of the Bull's Head, in Westgate, Bradford. A very nice establishment it is too. A good class of customer – artistic types, like yourself, sir. I would be right in thinking you're an artistic sort of person, would I, sir?'

'I suppose you could say so.'

'Ah, I thought so. It shows by the way you look at things, sir. You don't just gawp, but you look. Anyway, that was a lady as Lord Hertford went with for years. Not that she had sole rights in him, because I do know he had a son by a lady in Leeds at the time he was her protector – Leeds being closer, and more suitable for an evening's dalliance and home again to be let in by the night footman. But he was faithful to her in his fashion for a long time. Like I say, the great ones are different from us, even in their immoralities.'

Closer, it must be said, to people in artistic circles, though I myself have tried to shun the shoddy moral codes and practices of people in the theatre. 'And Lady Hertford? Does she have diversions of her own while they are in the North?'

'Not that we know of below stairs. And we would know. I would say Her Ladyship's taste is for Governance, and that's what she indulges in while she's in Yorkshire. And to do His Lordship proper credit, he lets her indulge it. Of course, it's her estate by inheritance, but there's many husbands who would have made sure they got the reins in their own hands. Whereas My Lord never interferes – there's many in this house as wish he did, because he's a bit less mean and a bit more fair. Not that we like him, but he's by far the lesser of two screws.'

124

'So you would hope that Her Ladyship maintains her hold on the King, whatever that hold may be?'

'Why do you say that? Is there some question of her losing it?'

'It is said he has found another Lady – Lady Conyngham – who can give him whatever it is he requires, though at a price – a price to the country. It could be Her Ladyship will spend less time at Court and more up here.'

'God help us! Except that there will be work. Her Ladyship always requires many servants about her.'

We passed incautiously into the next room, to find that we had caught up with the other party, who were being given a lengthy disquisition by the butler on the lineage of the Irvings, of whom Lady Hertford and her sisters were the last representatives. He looked up from his notes at our approach.

'Ah! Would you be Mr Mozart, sir? Yes? I reverence your genius, sir. We had "A Little Night Music" played in the courtyard here at Temple Newsam only last summer. And your arrangement of the *Messiah*! It fills me with admiration. After Handel . . . This will interest Mr Mozart, Thomas. You may go about your duties. Now, the seventh Viscount was yet another brother of . . .'

And I was forced to join the party and listen to a long account of Lady Hertford's family which no amount of narrative skill (and the butler had none) could make interesting. I gritted my teeth, but decided that I had had a fair amount of luck during my visit, and a fair amount of information.

That evening, round the fire, as the children were being put to their beds, my son Charles Thomas said:

'News of your visit is spreading, Father. I had a note this morning begging that you would give a concert of your music in Bradford. Shall I write and tell them that you are on holiday, and not here to give concerts?'

'Oh no,' I said expansively. 'I have quite a fancy to see Bradford. Tell them I'd be delighted.'

CHAPTER THIRTEEN
Lo Sposo Deluso

The concert in Bradford was a brilliant success. The advertisements, rushed out, spoke of 'The Foremost Musician of our Age' (so much for the Deaf Man of Vienna!) and the audience was large, attentive, and very musical. I played two of my Sonatas and many of my occasional pieces to rapturous applause, and at the end they demanded encore after encore, till I felt that they would never let me go.

'They like to get their money's worth in Yorkshire,' said my son, in that deflationary way children have with their parents.

Well, they certainly got their money's worth, but I was handsomely in pocket too, for it was a large hall, and the prices had been fixed with a view to bringing home to them that this was a once-in-a-lifetime experience. A London audience would have regarded that as a challenge, and would have stayed away. Bradford – all of polite Bradford, it seemed – took a different view, and came in their hundreds. I was sincerely complimentary to the gentlemen who had organised it.

'A most musical audience,' I said. 'As far removed from a London Society audience as it is possible to imagine.'

'Aye, we know a thing or two about music up t'North,' was the complacent reply from a large, heavy manufacturer. 'These London ladies and gentlemen, in my experience, know a little about a lot of things and not too much about anything.'

That did rather seem to sum them up.

'Now, you'll be wanting a spot of refreshment, Mr Mozart,' said another of the organisers.

'That would certainly be welcome.'

'Well, there's the Fly and Toad, the Emperor of Russia and the Bull's Head – they're all within walking distance, and they all do a very good spread.'

'I have heard good reports of the Bull's Head,' I said, and they nodded their heads and led the way there.

The Bull's Head turned out to be a handsome modern building in stone, most commodious in every respect. I could well believe it was the haunt of the artists and creative minds of the town, from the relaxed and congenial atmosphere in its bars, very different from the constrained and competitive feeling a tavern has when commercial and manufacturing men are its principal patrons. It was easy to pick out its landlady, for she had obviously bustled in from the concert a minute or two before, and was just come from the back where she had removed her coat. Now she was greeting other concert-goers from behind the bar.

She was a handsome, ample woman, red of face, sturdy of arm, and she exuded friendliness and good cheer – my ideal of a landlady, especially when combined with a willingness to extend credit. And that, if the Bull's Head was the resort of artists and writers, she must have been willing to do. She had a couple of young men with her behind the bar to enforce good order, but I did not imagine this was often a problem: her friendliness and firmness would together ensure that no one overstepped the mark. She kept her eye on the flow of people into the inn, and it was gratifying that when she saw us approaching the bar, and in particular myself, an expression of joyful surprise came over her face, and she could hardly express her pleasure.

'Oh! Good Heavens! Mr Mozart! Well, I could never have hoped . . . Oh, my good sir, what *pleasure* you have given us tonight, what heavenly pleasure!'

I must confess that, when I am received in this way, I wonder why I waste my days throwing my unregarded genius at the denizens of the capital. I made modest murmurs of demurral that were totally insincere, and made no objection when she insisted that I ate and drank that evening at her expense, as did all the gentlemen of the party, who had given Bradford the musical experience of a lifetime.

'It was the concert of one's dreams,' she said, seeming to babble away in her happiness; 'wonderful beyond our wildest expectations. And everybody in Bradford already worshipped you as the man who made the beautiful arrangement of the *Messiah!*'

'Bloody *Messiah!*' I roared.

I was conscious of a roomful of disapproving eyes fixed on me.

'I was talking to our delightful landlady about a most unsatisfactory performance of that masterpiece,' I lied hurriedly. 'In, er, Chiswick, I seem to remember. They had no idea of how that wonderful piece should go. No doubt you perform it with a proper reverence up North.'

'We do that,' said one of the manufacturers complacently.

I did not encourage further talk about *Messiah*. As the gentlemen of my party split up into groups, and my son went into earnest negotiations with a local mill-owner concerning music lessons for his daughters ('Music's not for boys, in my view, no disrespect intended, of course') I managed to get the good lady to myself, and was soon on an excellent footing with her. Before long we were seated in front of plates of rare beef, with roast potatoes, parsnips, carrots and horseradish sauce.

'I am not a glutton,' I said to my hostess, 'but you certainly know how to feed a man.'

'Get that into you, and then come back for more. My daughter says you're not a hearty eater. To tell you the truth she thinks you're vain about your figure.'

I let that last slander go, since I was bemused by her earlier remark. I gaped at her dumbly.

'Your daughter?'

'Oh, Mr Mozart, I beg your pardon! I thought that was why you were here – thought Betty must have told you to come here if you were in Bradford.'

128

'Betty? Then . . . then you are Mrs Ackroyd?'

She winked at me.

'Courtesy title. The nobility have them, so why shouldn't ordinary folk? Everybody calls me that, but there's never been a *Mr* Ackroyd. Saves a lot of questions and bother, and it looks better in a landlady who's trying to run a respectable establishment.'

'Of course, of course,' I said, my mind racing through a variety of possibilities. 'And of course it must have been better for little Betty not to be branded as—'

'A bastard?' She had lowered her voice, but was not embarrassed. 'Well, as to that, everybody *knew*. Because the fact is, Lord Hertford is a great man in the West Riding, and not much that he does can remain secret.' My mind stopped racing around and tried to come to terms with the astonishing truth as she went on: 'But as to being branded, there was really a lot of prestige, having such a great man as a father. My Betty would sometimes queen it over the other children as a little girl, though I spanked that out of her.'

'Was he fond of the child himself?'

She screwed up her face.

'My Lord? Oh, he's not a great one for fondness, nor for children either. He could be amused by her prattle for ten minutes, but then he'd have her taken away. He does his *duty* by people, does Lord H, but it's not often his emotions are involved.'

'No, that's my impression of the man.'

'He's patronising this opera season, isn't he?'

'Yes. Lord Hertford has always been a—' I was about to say 'generous' but substituted '*discriminating* patron of the musical theatre.'

Mrs Ackroyd smiled, and bent foward confidentially.

'Hot in bed and cold out of it – that's Lord Hertford. And I'm one who knows him.'

'I'm sure you are.'

'And he'll be a bit past the "bed" thing by now, I'd reckon.'

'Certainly one hears no rumours around the theatres.'

'What has replaced it, I wonder? Something always does,

you know, when powerful lust fades away. Would it be wealth, perhaps? Or power?'

'The two things rather go together,' I said. 'I think he and his wife are very interested in both of them.'

'Then perhaps they are closer now than they ever were in my time. If rumour is true they both of them batten powerfully on the new King.'

'Certainly they have done for years. But if London rumour is correct their time is drawing to a close.'

She nodded, obviously enjoying this gossip about Great Ones she had known, in her time, more intimately than anyone. 'Yes, I had heard that from Betty. King's favourite is a thankless position, isn't it? Anyone who loses favour is quickly out in the cold.'

The relevance to her own position may have struck her. She bustled about to refill our plates and glasses, though I tried to stop her.

'Nonsense,' she said. 'You're in Yorkshire, and you'll eat as a Yorkshireman does.'

When we had settled down over our victuals once more, I said:

'As far as you are concerned Lord Hertford has exercised his power beneficently?'

'Oh yes. I'd never say otherwise.'

'And as far as Betty is concerned too?'

'Certainly. Neither of us has any complaint.'

'How did she get her musical education?'

'Through His Lordship.' She sat back in the inn's settle. 'Well, what happened was, I started noticing that she had what seemed to me a lovely voice, but being an ignorant woman I didn't trust myself, so I took her along to our vicar, Mr Morgan. Being Welsh he's very musical – and precious long-winded too, but maybe that's from the same cause. Anyway, he's a kindly person, and mostly never mentions my past history. Well, he heard her, and he said he'd never heard a voice like it, and he said: "Mrs Ackroyd, it's your duty to get that voice trained." '

'He was right.'

'Any road, I had a word with the steward from Temple Newsam next time he came calling, as he regularly did on orders from Lord H., and he put in a word with his master and – well, to cut a long story short, when he was convinced that what we were saying was nothing less than the truth, he sent her to the best teacher in Bradford. He often made enquiries about her progress, and once sent word by the steward that he regarded the voice lessons as an excellent investment.'

'A touch cold, but at least he was willing to stand by his investment.'

'Oh, he was. He sent her on a tour of the Continent, so she would be ahead of other young singers in her knowledge of all the latest fashions and trends.' Rossini. That's what *that* meant. 'Oh no, we've no complaints, Betty or I, about His Lordship.'

'And now he is furthering her career in London?'

'Exactly. What more could Betty have asked for? Of course I had my doubts about her setting off in life on her own so young, but it had to happen some time, and with a gift like that I would never have been able to keep her in Bradford.'

'Oh, I'm sure you did right. I am a little surprised that Betty never told me that Lord Hertford is her father.'

She laid down her knife and fork, and looked at me open-mouthed.

'You mean you didn't *know*? Oh Mr Mozart, I *am* ashamed! Here's me rattling on about my private affairs convinced you already knew all about them!'

'It's been most interesting. I care deeply for Betty and for her talent. Is there any reason why she should have kept her parentage quiet?'

She shrugged.

'Everybody knows here ... I suppose, maybe, that making a fresh start in London, she thought it wasn't everybody's business to comment on her family background.'

'Or possibly Lord Hertford asked her to keep it quiet?'

'That's possible. Him being such a party man, so much of a Tory, maybe he felt it would harm her career, particularly at the present time. If he did ask her she'd have agreed. She knows she's much in his debt.'

131

'For life itself.'

'Oh yes, but children always forget that, don't they?'

'Not my own, I am happy to say,' I said, nodding towards my dear son. 'Does she feel any . . . love for him?'

'Oh, I don't think so. How could she, when she never knew him all the time she was growing up, not to remember? But respect. It's worked out a lot better with him and me and her than in some other cases.'

'Oh? Other cases around here?'

She smiled and drank a healthy swig of porter.

'I never was the only one. Even in my time there were others.'

'I heard about a lady friend in Leeds.'

'That was who I was thinking about, where it didn't work out so well, not by a long chalk. I never met her, but I've been told she was a very beautiful woman, and much more of a lady than I ever was. I think she managed things less well than I did, but, thinking about it, maybe there wasn't much else she could do.'

'Was it a different situation?'

'It was. She was married, you see.'

'Ah.'

'Married to a gentleman who was quite prosperous in the Manchester trade. Had a big shop in Briggate, and a very good class of customer. She was childless and interested in charitable work among the poor and homeless. When the liaison began – I don't know how or when it started – he rented a small apartment on the outskirts of Leeds so they could be together whenever he pleased. As far as the husband was concerned she was about her charitable business – which very often she *was*, so there was not much danger of being found out. The husband himself was often away on business – buying, visiting mills and so on – so all in all she must have felt herself quite safe.'

'What went wrong?'

'She found herself in an interesting condition.'

'Ah.'

'And of course being in her way a devout person she would not commit the sin of having an abortion, though

132

there were plenty in Leeds could have helped her to one.'

'She was married – was it a great problem?'

'Oh, she herself was uncertain who the father was, but the likelihood was, since she and her husband had been childless for nearly ten years, that it was Lord Hertford. Now as you know Lord Hertford is a very dark man – dark hair, dark complexion, what they call saturnine.'

'I remember when he was. He's quite white of hair now.'

'Of course he would be. I suppose it makes him look less forbidding. Now the husband was very fair of skin and blond of hair – something of the Viking there, I suppose, for many of his family were the same. So even before the birth she began dropping hints that *her* father was very dark of hair and complexion, though she herself was auburn.'

'Was her father dead?'

'No, he'd had a financial collapse and had taken himself and his family to the Continent, to Germany, where they could live very respectably on very little. They'd been there for years, and Lord Hertford's mistress, who was the eldest daughter, was the only one who had remained behind, being a teacher in a respectable school. Anyway, the boy was born, dark of hair and of skin, and the husband didn't think twice, except to make the odd joke as fathers do. He was pleased as Punch and proud of the boy. He was a stern man, but quite good in his heart. Or perhaps I should say "just" – it's not quite the same thing, is it?'

I nodded my understanding.

'What happened?'

'The Peace of Amiens. People in England thought the wars were at an end and set out to travel on the Continent. Nobody there thought they were over, and many of the English took the opportunity to return home. So one day in 1802 there on the doorstep was her father, large as life and ginger of hair. *And* his family, ranging from the auburn to the flaming red. The husband was very stern, very controlled, but before a week had gone by he'd had the truth out of her.'

'What did he do?'

133

'He couldn't bear the thought of living with someone who'd deceived him for so long. He wasn't ungenerous – far from it in the circumstances. He set the father up in business in a small way in Dewsbury, and sent his wife off with them. But he kept the boy with him in Leeds.'

'That was hard.'

'Was it? Hard on the wife, perhaps, but not on the son. He believed in punishing the guilty, but not the innocent. He loved him as a son and brought him up as a son, and he had every advantage. His business later went into a bit of a decline, but he's still alive, living in a modest way. No, I don't criticise him, though there's many do.'

'Why?'

'He brought up the son to hate the father. I don't know when he told him he *was* his father, but he told him Lord Hertford had betrayed his mother and he passed on his own bitter, bitter hatred to the boy. There's some that say that's unnatural.'

'It's certainly . . . unattractive.'

She shook her head, unwilling to go along with that.

'We're good haters up here in Yorkshire. We have a saying around here: "Keep a stone in thy pocket seven year; turn it, and keep it seven year longer, that it may be ever ready to thine hand when thine enemy draws near." He would have said *he* was the boy's father in everything except an accident of nature, and he had a right to teach him to hate anyone who'd injured him.'

'You obviously are on the man's side.'

'Oh, I am.' She got up and began collecting up plates. 'Though to be honest I sometimes thank my stars I was never married, particularly to someone as bitter and unbending as Mr Hartshead.'

CHAPTER FOURTEEN
E Quello è Mio Padre

The rest of my stay was uneventful, and was spent mainly in the happy home in Wakefield. On the journey back to London through the paddy fields of Lincolnshire I had much to meditate on: the happiness of the little family I had just left; the fact that I had invited to the first performance of my new opera *Le Comari Allegre di Windsor* not only my son, but his wife and children as well (how were they to be accommodated?); and, most insistently, the facts I had learnt about the birth and backgrounds of Betty Ackroyd and Bradley Hartshead.

I reviewed in my mind the facts. Both the young people were the bastard offspring of Lord Hertford. At some stage since coming to London – or possibly on the continent – they had joined forces, and this fact Betty had not told her mother, though obviously she had told her a good deal about me. The possibility that the pair had conceived a plot to discredit or ruin their natural father was surely a real one. I discounted any idea that that plot could have involved murder: I did *not* believe either of them capable of that, nor yet both together. But thinking back to the ineffectual figure of Jenny Bowles I did wonder if she had somehow blundered into her murder, if it had been almost unintentional, but brought about by her own inadequacy or muddleheadedness.

I thought over what I knew about Bradley Hartshead – very much less than I knew about Betty. I had never seen him behave towards Lord Hertford with anything other than the impeccable courtesy which the man himself would enforce. But then I had not very often seen them together at all. I was beginning to rely on Hartshead as a sympathetic figure, an admirer of my music, and an extremely competent musician. I was thinking of him as a helper in the preparation of *Le Comari Gaie di Windsor* – yes, that would be better: *gaie*. I did not want to forego his assistance either because of opposition from Lord Hertford or because the young man did not want any association with his father. But then I had seen no suspicion of either emotion in either of the men.

I wondered how things were going at the Queen's trial. My son did not take a newspaper and I had been too busy and happy to borrow one. What was more, people had not been talking about it. Was this because interest was declining, or because people in the North regard doings in the South of the country with the sort of scorn they also pour on the doings of foreigners? I thought it probable that things were now nearing a conclusion and there was now no question of the King's party changing their mind and producing Betty Ackroyd as 'Jenny'. Did this mean that things would have calmed down and there was no longer any danger (if there ever had been any) to Davy? Pleasant though the lad's company was in the apartment I had no desire to imprison him. Even if the danger had receded it might be advisable to send him back to Essex, or even up to the North, though not to anywhere within Lord Hertford's sphere of influence. But the North is indeed another country, and I couldn't see Davy working in one of the hellish mills there.

I left the coach, stiff and weary, at the Queen's Head, in the Strand. It was early afternoon. I found a fellow to carry my luggage up to Henrietta Street, and I was just paying him off on the landing outside my apartment when I thought I heard sounds from inside. Cautiously opening the door, fearful of what might be being done to Davy, I stood for a moment listening. I was shocked and horrified to hear shouts and cries of pleasure from the direction of the small bedroom. There was no question whose was the man's voice, and a moment's listening convinced me that the woman's was my little servant Ann's (not, you

136

understand, that I had ever before heard her in that situation).

I was, as I say, shocked. I felt awkward, however, about interrupting the guilty pair. I tried also to remember Davy's lonely and dangerous situation. I pulled my travelling trunk through the door, took off my heavy coat and put it on top of it, then left the apartment for the theatre.

The piece for that evening, I found out when I arrived, was once again *The Call to Arms*, which I was assured was still attracting good audiences. I was pleased, because it meant that Betty Ackroyd was in the theatre. I was still more pleased when I found out from a member of the orchestra that Bradley Hartshead was now directing some performances from the fortepiano, and was doing so that evening. I went to my little office (a mere broom-cupboard), and, trying to put the business of Jenny's murder from my mind, I wrote to the divine Therese suggesting that we should resume our musical work together now that I had returned from the North. Then I went up to see Betty Ackroyd.

She had now, I was pleased to see, got her own dresser, and a real one: a strong, heavy, capable woman whose first words revealed her to be a Yorkshirewoman. I was pleased to see this acknowledgement of Betty's position in the theatre but the woman did, being an unknown quantity and by no means inclined to make herself scarce, place some restrictions on our conversation.

Betty beamed her welcome.

'I hear you gave a concert in Bradford, and that it was a great success,' she said.

'It was. The audience seemed much more discriminating than I'm used to in London.'

'They are. My mother was in a seventh heaven at having met and talked with you.'

'A most impressive woman,' I said, coming to sit on the rickety structure that was dignified by the term dressing table. 'You are lucky in your parentage.'

'Do you think so?'

'I must confess one part of it came as a surprise,' I said, with a meaningful look.

'I'm glad to hear it,' she said, not batting an eyelid. 'And I trust you will not surprise anybody else with the information.'

'Of course I won't,' I agreed readily. 'Still, it seems very generally known in Bradford. How can what is common gossip in Bradford remain secret in London?'

'In the same way as what is common gossip in Abyssinia is totally unknown in London. We are talking, my dear Mr Mozart, of two different worlds.'

I raised my eyebrows sceptically.

'And yet you, my dear, have gone from one to the other, and My Lord goes constantly between, and to other worlds represented by his own estates. We are not talking about separate prisons to which the keys have been lost. People move, people travel. And when Mr Stephenson's excellent invention is perfected we shall have people drawn by steam along the roads the length and breadth of the kingdom.'

'I believe it will need rails,' she said pedantically. 'And I am not talking about ten or twenty years in the future. I am talking about now. *Now* I do not want my career in the theatre to spring from anything but my own voice, my own musicianship, my own talent for the stage. Surely you can understand that, Mr Mozart?'

'Certainly I can understand it.'

'I will not have it said I have been foisted on the public by any of the great ones in the land. I will not be championed by this party or that for reasons that have nothing to do with music. Above all I do not want it said that my path was somehow made easy. If it becomes known when I am famous whose daughter I am – so be it. I shall have done everything by my own efforts.'

I could not but applaud her resolution.

'Your determination does you credit. I assure you that no one shall hear anything about your background from me.'

'Make sure they don't!'

'Trust me, my dear. Have you ever heard it said that I'm a gossip?'

'Yes.'

'Well, I don't know what can have led anyone to say

138

that . . .' Honesty compelled me to examine myself, and I amended this. 'Of course I do enjoy a good story.'

'Of course you do. You've been chuckling over stories about the Queen for months, and passing them on. And I've heard you telling tales about Signor Rossini's amorous entanglements when you couldn't possibly know whether they were true or false. Mark this: I want nothing said about this matter, Mr Mozart.'

'Nothing will be.'

'Silent as the grave.'

This reminded us both of a certain watery grave, and we exchanged looks. I kissed her and left the dressing-room. It occurred to me that when Betty *did* become famous, under her own or some manufactured foreign name, she was going to be a very formidable prima donna indeed.

By now the messenger had returned with a reply from the beautiful Brunswicker, and it was given to me by one of the Queen's Theatre's attendants. It was a brief note, but scented, and redolent of her.

'My dear Master,' it read in German,

I am desolated to find that I have no free mornings for the next ten days. I am much in demand at Court, where my dear husband is also much appreciated for his reminiscences of the allies' victories over the Corsican tyrant. Be assured that when I am free I shall summon you so that I may hear again from the Fountainhead how to interpret your so heavenly music.

Until then,
Therese

I confess that this note dissatisfied me, if anything that divine creature might do could dissatisfy me. There seemed to be a preference for a life in Society over a life of music that I should have thought no properly constituted mind could entertain. And the picture of her bear of a husband inflicting his guttural war memoirs on the Court at Windsor made me almost feel sorry for Prinny, whose impeccable if superficial courtesy must have been tested to

139

the uttermost. This all seemed to denote an *imperfection* in my lovely singer, a failure of taste and judgment. God knows, though, I should have got used to imperfections and failures of taste in singers over the years.

I was pondering this unsatisfactory missive in the foyer when Mr Popper bustled up, his turkey-cock strut and puffed-out cheeks all the more irritating for my having been among people of genuine taste since I last saw him.

'Ah, Mr Mozart – you are back at last.'

'As you see.'

'Lord Hertford was none too pleased that you left town without informing him.'

'I didn't know I was expected to.'

'Heavens above! Artists, artists!'

Mr Popper is always trying to convey the idea that he is a man of business. In fact he couldn't have run a pawn-broker's in Shoreditch, even if he gave his whole mind to it. The truth is there are artists who create, artists who interpret, and a great public which wants what the artists provide. The Poppers of this world are at best middle men, at worst irrelevancies.

'I am of course at His Lordship's service.'

(At a price. Definitely a price.)

'Well, there have been developments. I shall say no more than that.' (He didn't know any more than that.) 'I will inform His Lordship of your return.'

'Don't trouble yourself. I shall not be directing the performance tonight. I am too tired after travelling. I will write the note to Lord Hertford myself.'

'Make it very respectful, Mr Mozart. His Lordship was decidedly discomposed.'

'I know the ways of the world, Mr Popper.'

In other words I can grovel as well as the next man when I have a mind to. I composed a suitable note, comprising equal parts of *peccavi* and nauseating foot-licking, and dispatched it by the usual messenger (who haunts the Haymarket and makes a few pennies a day carrying the *billets doux* and requests for financial assistance that issue from the theatres there). When I came back into the Queen's Bradley Hartshead was there waiting for me.

140

'Mr Mozart, welcome back!'

'Mr Hartshead. I hear you have done sterling work in my absence. I am grateful and pleased.'

'It has been a great joy. I know your opinion of *The Call to Arms*—' I gave the piece a gesture of dismissal with my hand—'but perhaps I can regard it as a sort of preparation for directing *Figaro* or *The Enchanted Violin*.'

I regarded him with affection.

'I am glad you appreciate the latter. It was described to me not long ago as "something light". It still rankles.'

'I hear the North has shown better appreciation of your genius.'

'It has.'

'It would. It's no surprise to a Northerner like me.'

'Still, I wish they wouldn't keep mentioning *Messiah* . . .'

Hartshead laughed.

'It's the Northern equivalent of Midnight Mass on Christmas Eve for Catholics. No – it's more than that: it's a national and regional celebration as well as a religious one. My father used to take me every year, and it impressed on me the glory of being an Englishman and a Yorkshireman.'

I looked the scepticism I felt.

'You must excuse a mere foreigner from trying to understand how a piece by a German can do that. Is your father still alive?'

He answered unconstrainedly.

'Yes, but old and frail. He has a small house in Guiseley, near Leeds. He is not as prosperous in his retirement as he and I hoped, but business in his last years as a Manchester merchant was poor. The Orders in Council hit everyone in the cotton trade, as you know.'

'Indeed they did. Well, it was a happy visit, but coming back I find that I have been a naughty boy.'

'Oh?'

'I have missed . . . developments. Need I say more? I am going home now to my own bed and a well-earned sleep. Could you give a message to Betty for me please?'

'Of course.'

I deliberately at this point feigned to be looking out to

141

the street, though from the corner of my eye I could still see his face.

'Would you tell her that there may be another conference tomorrow? At Hertford House, of course. Lord Hertford will send a message to her.'

I do not think I was mistaken in seeing a fleeting look come into Bradley Hartshead's eyes at the mention of the man – a look of virulent hatred.

'I'll give her the message,' he said neutrally.

When I got home I found Davy very subdued. There was no sign of Ann, but she would ordinarily have gone home by then. Davy had unpacked my trunk, and had the wherewithal for a simple meal for me. I ate the beefsteak and boiled potatoes and carrots, rather well cooked and served: the boy learnt fast. I drank a pint of claret, and when I pushed away my plate I called Davy in and gestured him to sit opposite me.

'Davy, I was sorry to hear what I did when I arrived home.'

He was wringing his hands nervously under the table.

'I thought as how you must have heard. I'm sorry, Mr Mozart. I was so lonely, and felt so frightened. It was as if I hadn't much life left, and ought . . . well, like to take any chances there were.'

'That's a poor excuse for debauching a young girl.'

'Oh, I wasn't the first, sir.'

'That is no excuse either. You took advantage of my absence and her unprotected state. Think of the plight of the poor girl if she should find herself with child.'

He smiled slowly.

'Oh, that won't happen, sir. Trust me! I know a thing or two!'

What, I asked myself, is the world coming to? I dismissed him to his bed and went most unhappily to mine.

CHAPTER FIFTEEN
Sinfonia Concertante

'Ah, Mr Mozart.'

There are ways of saying 'Ah, Mr Mozart', ranging from the enthusiastic and welcoming to the disapproving, disappointed, unimpressed, and all sorts of other words mostly beginning with dis- or un-. The weathervane of Mr de Fries's tone was pointing unmistakably in the latter direction. Mr Popper, already seated on a gilded chair that ministered to his self-importance, gave me a look which said 'I told you so'. I bowed generally and took another of the chairs. Coffee and biscuits were there on a tray on the table, but no attempt was made to serve us any.

I had been summoned by a brief note sent to my apartment that morning. It was unquestionably a summons rather than an invitation. I was clear in my mind that I was going to have to do something to retrieve my position with Lord Hertford but, not knowing what had come up in my absence to make my presence at his beck and call so desirable, it was impossible to plan how to do this.

Betty's arrival was immediately followed by that of Lord Hertford. No doubt the footman had told him we were now all assembled. He walked in more haltingly than usual – doubtless an attack of gout or arthritis – and his face was sometimes visited by grimaces of pain. I sometimes forget how *old* a man he is. He retained something still, however, of his usual affable manner.

'Miss Ackroyd – good to see you! Your common sense will be invaluable. Good day, Mr Popper. Ah, Mr Mozart.'

I bowed. He eased himself into a seat and gestured to us to sit down. Mr de Fries began dispensing coffee. Servants were clearly not wanted, even during the preliminaries. The organisation of the refreshments took some minutes, but Lord Hertford did not try to lighten the atmosphere by making trivial conversation. He certainly did not ask me if I had had an enjoyable stay in the North.

When we all had our coffee and biscuit he opened the matter without preamble.

'I have not asked you here today to revise or reverse decisions made when we all met three weeks ago. The time when Miss Ackroyd could have impersonated Jenny Bowles before the House of Lords is now, I am afraid, past. Things are drawing to a close there. I am happy to say I am beginning to detect a turning of the tide of popular sentiment in the King's direction.'

'Really?' I said incautiously. 'I didn't get any such feeling in the North.'

Teeth were shown.

'But I am not talking about the North, Mr Mozart. How could popular feeling swing first in the North when the King and the . . . er, Princess are both in London?'

'True, of course,' I murmured pacifyingly.

'And I think I can say that I – Mr de Fries and I – have had something to do with this turning of the tide.'

'Indeed?' said Mr Popper, as if preparing to be enormously impressed.

Lord Hertford nodded, preparing to impress.

'Yes. You remember something was said about starting rumours – reminds me of that delightful piece by Rossini, eh, Mr Mozart? – something about rumours last time we gathered here, and I rather pooh-poohed the idea. But the suggestion – yours, Mr Popper, I think – set Mr de Fries here thinking. He is a man of great resource – may I say cunning, Mr de Fries?'

'I should be flattered, My Lord.'

Well, he was paid to fawn, of course.

'So, having thought and discussed the matter with me, he decided to have the rumours started by some low fellows we hired in the ale-houses and taverns in the vicinity of Alderman Wood's house. We made the rumours accord most exactly with what we had been told by Jenny Bowles: date, time of evening, the details of the conversation overheard, and so on. This meant that when the servants of the Alderman came in and were confronted with these rumours, they denied them, of course, but in so shuffling and embarrassed a way that they as good as confirmed them. De Fries argued to himself that the likelihood was that one or some of the servants knew. And if some did, all did. And he was right – proved right by their reactions. So the rumours started on their way with a very much firmer base than most of the rumours about the Queen. Er, the Princess.'

'Brilliant!' said Mr Popper. 'And it makes me proud that I – that a suggestion by me—'

'Yes, yes, Mr Popper. You have been as always most useful. We meditate now trying to find the actual watermen who – who were used, and perhaps giving their names to the less scrupulous public prints. The *Observer* would publish it with no hesitation I feel sure. But all this is by the way. It is not what I have called you here for today.'

He paused. Mr Popper tried to look serious and intelligent.

'I have had a communication—'

Lord Hertford gestured with his hand towards Mr de Fries, who shook his head.

'I don't have it, My Lord. I took it to the graphologist as you asked me to.'

'Of course. No matter. It was short enough. I'm sure you can retail the contents word for word.'

'I think I can, My Lord. The note read: "Where did you bury the body of the poor girl? And what is the price of silence?" That was all.'

There was a complete hush in the room. This was the sort of development that probably most of us had feared. Everyone was thinking the matter through and regretting that they themselves were implicated.

'It sounds like the beginning of blackmail,' said Mr Popper.

145

'Brilliant!' said Lord Hertford. He immediately seemed to regret his sharpness. 'I'm sorry, my dear sir. I do apologise. I forget that you haven't had the time that we have had to ponder the note. Yes, it does indeed look like the prelude to an attempt at blackmail.'

'How was the note delivered?' asked Betty.

'Uncertain, because my damned footman is getting too old for his duties. He says he *thinks* it was handed in by a young female. But of course that young female will not prove to be the writer of the note.'

'Of course not. When was this?'

'Five days ago.'

'What did the handwriting look like?' I asked.

'To me unremarkable,' said Mr de Fries. 'As I say I took it only this morning to a woman specialising in the study of handwriting – someone highly recommended by Lady Hertford herself. We will await the fruits of her study. Her initial reactions were that the writer was educated, probably male or a very strong-willed female, one dominated by love of or desire for money, probably a Libra subject. Those were her first thoughts.'

My eyes strayed to Lord Hertford. He was a man who seemed never to have been attracted by what I would call a truly womanly woman. I did have doubts about the advice of his particularly strong-willed female on this question. I wondered how far I could go in voicing them. Finally I coughed.

'My Lord, I have no wish to cast doubt on Lady Hertford's advice—'

'I'm sure you *have*n't, Mr Mozart.'

'—but I wonder a little about the woman you are consulting about this note.'

'Her discretion is guaranteed, Mr Mozart,' said Lord Hertford, unbending a little. 'She has been consulted by the King himself on a number of delicate matters.'

'It was not her discretion I was questioning, My Lord. I was wondering whether hers was the kind of *scientific* analysis and report that would be useful to us. Is hers, for example, the sort of expert judgment that the authorities might solicit and bring forward at a criminal trial (which of

146

course is what the matter could one day come to)?'

'I hope *not*, Mr Mozart,' said Lord Hertford emphatically.

'Of course we will all hope not, My lord. But what I mean is that I suspect if I had seen the note I might have recognised the hand of an educated person rather than someone who had been a year or two at Dame School. I think I would have had a better than even chance of guessing whether it was the hand of a man or a woman. I think the content would have told me that the writer was interested in money, and as to the writer being a Libra subject – are we really in this day and age to give credence to the nonsense spouted by astrologers?'

I had perhaps not put the matter as tactfully as I might, but Lord Hertford did not appear, at any rate, to take it amiss, at least not on the surface.

'I'm surprised at you, Mr Mozart,' he said genially, but not able to mask an underlying coldness in his reactions to me. 'You and I belong to an organisation – a brotherhood, let us call it – which alerts us to the forces above and beyond the rationalities of this world. It astonishes me that an artist such as yourself should be so earth-bound as your words seem to imply.'

'I merely mean that if we are to find out who is attempting to commit this crime of blackmail I should be sorry to have to resort to occult sources rather than the sources that might be of use on our side in a Court of Law.'

Lord Hertford shook his head.

'I have no intention of letting this matter come to a Court of Law, Mr Mozart. It would do you – and me – no good at all. But tell us what you would do, faced with this threat.'

I felt unpleasantly exposed.

'I would think, My Lord. What does this note tell us? That the writer is someone who knows that you – we – got rid of a body. He doesn't know how or where, or he would not have used the word "buried". Therefore we must posit a second person in the street, watching the theatre as Davy House was watching it, or someone in the buildings around the Queen's Theatre, or – and this is the solution I

147

would suggest is the most likely – someone in the theatre itself.'

They all looked at me thoughtfully.

'Go on,' said Lord Hertford.

'If we can imagine that someone in the theatre that night killed poor Jenny, we can also imagine that someone in the theatre came upon her body in Miss Ackroyd's dressing-room. There may have been reasons why that person did not raise the alarm, or there may have been none beyond a desire not to be involved in all the fuss of a murder and the pursuit of its perpetrator. But the person could have waited concealed inside the theatre – or indeed watched from outside or from a building in the vicinity – and seen the body transported away clandestinely. And one of the people involved in this clandestine work was you, My Lord – one of the richest men in the kingdom. He – or she – may have found the opportunity this presented for blackmail irresistible.'

There was another long silence. They gave the impression of being impressed.

'By someone in the theatre,' began Betty, 'you mean—?'

'Any of the artists or stage-hands, any of the orchestra, the dressers, and any of the audience.'

'You think a member of the audience is really a possibility?' asked Lord Hertford, thoughtfully.

'I do. During a performance there is, regrettably from the performers' point of view, a great deal of toing and froing in and out of the auditorium. People leave early, bladders and bowels have to be eased, some even, I fear, have assignations back stage with members of the cast.'

'I can't remember much toing and froing,' said Lord Hertford. 'People were enjoying it so much.'

'Perhaps, My Lord, you were enjoying it so much – I hope so – that you failed to notice.'

'Possibly, possibly . . . Capital little piece.' That, I recognised, was a sop thrown in my direction. 'The question is: what do we do?'

We all looked at each other.

'I'm not sure there is much we can do until His Lordship receives a second note,' I said. 'I presume the footmen will

148

this time be on the alert?'

'They will,' said Lord Hertford grimly.

'However, if I was a blackmailer I would use a different method of delivery and a different hand in the addressing, so the alertness may not be of much use. I wonder if Miss Ackroyd could be of some use – and Mr Popper too, of course – in finding out if anyone saw anything unusual, or more especially any unexpected *person*, backstage at the Queen's on the first night of *A Call to Arms*. I have tried myself, but to little avail.'

Betty Ackroyd looked dubious.

'Everyone was buoyed up by the success of it,' she said. 'One wasn't noticing much outside the piece itself. But I can try.'

'We are interested particularly in the area around the dressing-rooms,' I went on. 'Particularly your own.'

'Particularly mine,' agreed Betty.

'You might pretend to have lost something that night – that is the sort of simple reason for questioning that everyone understands. We want to know about anybody who was seen in that vicinity during the second act.'

'If anyone can find out anything to the purpose I'm sure it will be Miss Ackroyd,' said Lord Hertford. 'Well, I think we've gone as far as we *can* go today . . .'

He rose. It was a dismissal, but he was quite right: there was nothing to do but wait. I noted, however, that he had accepted my analysis of the situation, as well as my suggestion for future action. As we all collected ourselves together and made our ways out he came over to me with an access of that old geniality that I could no longer take at its face value.

'Ah, my dear Mozart, I hear you visited my wife's old home while you were up in the North.'

'I did, er, take that opportunity, My Lord. And I'm very glad that I did. It is indeed a most splendid property.'

'We have a great deal of music when we are up there. You must come up and play for us some time. You were treated well, I trust?'

'Oh indeed. I had a most interesting tour of the main rooms. Her Ladyship's butler was most interesting on the various members of the Ingram family and their fortunes.'

'Ha! *Flaneur!* Admit it, Mr Mozart: you were bored to death!' He bared his teeth at me. 'We lay him on to deter the tourists.'

We were out in the splendid corridor. He raised his hand to me and hobbled away.

Once out in the dreary November sunlight I looked around me. Mr Popper had secured a cab and was speeding on his way, presumably to create chaos at the Queen's. On the corner of Baker Street I spied Betty Ackroyd, and I saw that she had been waited for by Bradley Hartshead. The two of them were close together, heads down, in deep conversation. Then they turned and began the long walk in the direction of Soho.

I strolled behind them, cursing the inveterate damp cold of these isles, letting them exhaust the topic of blackmail, if that was what they were talking about. Whatever it was seemed to interest them: their heads remained together and they were talking low. It was not until they were in the splendid curve of Regent Street – built, the wags said to mirror the curve of Prinny's stomach – that I decided it was time for them and me to have a chat.

'And have you reached any conclusions?' I said, coming up beside them. They looked at me apparently unsurprised.

'I've been trying to persuade Betty to have as little as possible to do with this business,' said Bradley Hartshead without hesitation. 'But she says she's now in it so deep that it would be pointless to withdraw.'

'I'm afraid that that's true of many of us,' I replied. 'We both should have drawn back the moment we heard Jenny Bowles's story, saying this was a matter for politicians, not artists. And you two should most certainly not have got yourselves involved in this impersonation scheme.'

'Money,' said Betty Ackroyd. 'It's the usual thing. The gift Lord Hertford offered seemed to give me everything I wanted: more travel, seeing continental opera houses, maybe singing there, learning my trade in Italy or Germany.'

'It's the downfall of all of us,' I agreed. 'I wanted to

ensure Lord Hertford's support for the opera season, and in particular for *Le Comari di Windsor*.'

'Is that what it's called now?'

'At the moment. I feel there must be something still shorter and livelier.'

'Anyway, in the event there was no impersonation, no great sum of money from Lord Hertford, and *The Call to Arms* seems to have done more for my career than His Lordship's money could do.'

I nodded sagely.

'That's right: rely on your artistry for your own artistic advancement.' Seeing a satiric look on her face I added: 'I wish I could claim to have done so in my own life.'

'Perhaps you preferred not to starve,' said Betty. We all laughed.

'Mr Mozart is right, and he would never have starved,' said Hartshead. 'He would merely have lived less well.'

'Is "well" how I have lived?' I mused. 'It doesn't seem so to me. But without aristocratic help now and again I certainly would have had less time to write my *real* music.' I turned to look Bradley Hartshead in the eye. 'And have you enjoyed the patronage of Lord Hertford?'

'No.'

It was said stony-faced.

'Then it was a pity you connived in the impersonation of poor Jenny.'

'It was, even though Lord Hertford knows nothing of my small involvement. It was very foolish of me. But Betty was so set on it.'

'Betty takes a very different view of your father to your own.'

They both turned on me, then Betty looked down, took Bradley Hartshead's arm, and we all walked along in silence for a minute or two.

'I suppose it was my foolish mother who told you,' said Betty bitterly.

'Your excellent mother told me the story merely to illustrate the fate of a woman who was similarly involved with Lord Hertford but was less fortunate than herself. She knows, I would guess, nothing of Mr Hartshead here.

151

If anyone was foolish it was surely you for not mentioning him.'

Again we walked on in silence, eventually broken by Bradley Hartshead.

'What I said was true, Mr Mozart: I have never accepted anything in the way of help or patronage from Lord Hertford.'

'A good thing, in my view, since the rumour is that you hate him.'

He gave a gesture of contempt with his free hand.

'Local gossip. I was brought up to detest his name. That was my father's view of him, and I respected it, and still do. But that was one of the childish things I put from me when I became a man. My mother behaved no worse than many women, and Lord Hertford behaved no worse than many aristocrats. Or many mill-owners, come to that.'

'And you get on well with him?'

'I have as little to do with him as possible. I cannot pretend to like him.'

'Why not?'

'He has no heart. Have you ever found one?'

'Never. If he gives, it is for a reason. Happily it is sometimes an *artistic* reason, and I have benefited from that. What is his feeling for you?'

'I have no idea. I have never in my life talked to him alone. I suspect he is amused in a lofty way that two of his bastards have become musicians. He prides himself on his taste.'

'Justly. But this taste would be still better if he had a heart. And how did the brother and sister find each other?'

A sort of shutter came over Hartshead's face.

'Oh, that's easily told: I was accompanying on the organ at a performance of – if you'll pardon my naming it – *Messiah* in Chiswick. A small parish church affair, a year or so ago. Betty was singing soprano.'

We were nearing Betty's lodging now. As we approached it, taking advantage of a part of the street that was deserted, Betty turned and put her hand on my hand.

'That was how we *met*, Mr Mozart. When you meet you

do not talk immediately of your parentage, and certainly not truthfully if you are in our position. That we only talked of months later. And by then we . . . things had taken place between us that made it impossible for us to be *simply* brother and sister.'

'That is why we wish to go abroad,' said Bradley, sadly. 'We need to go somewhere where we are not known, and where our parentage is of no interest to anyone.'

Then they walked off with dignity to Betty's – to their – lodging.

CHAPTER SIXTEEN
Così Fan Tutte

I sometimes wonder whether it is a good thing for a composer to live to old age. I think of Mr Purcell, the closest thing to a musical genius ever produced by this fog-mantled kingdom. He died young, and everyone regrets the masterpieces he never lived to produce. Nobody will ever bemoan the masterpieces I never lived to produce. I've produced them all, and precious little have they been appreciated. If it were not for the good Mr Novello many of them would hardly be worth the music paper they are written on. Even if my new opera is produced and is a success, its fate will probably be to be plundered to furnish a 'version' by Mr Bishop which will have a few of my best arias together with many others plundered from Arne, Storace and Bishop himself, and probably 'The Jolly Ploughboy' and 'Drink to Me Only' to boot. Is it all worth it, I ask myself?

This feeling was brought on when I arrived home to find a splendid invitation card awaiting me: it was to a party at Lord Egremere's. At one time my heart would have beat faster: the chance to meet the great ones of this little world of England, the opportunity to cultivate their favour, perhaps to borrow off them. Now . . . Well, no doubt I would do all those things, but routinely, with a sense of ennui. My life was nearly over, I was seen by many as a musical hack, I had shot my bolt.

Except for my new opera.

Even as depression seemed to settle on me, my spirits rose at the thought of it. What a wonderful score it was, in spite of its libretto. And what a chance this was! I had heard whispers of Lord Egremere's approaching party. The rumour-mongers had it that Prinny was going to be there, and that it was going to represent a tentative hand of friendship from him to the Whigs. Relations between them had been sulphurous since he had ditched his old friends and allies on becoming Regent a decade ago. For Prinny treachery was a way of life, to be practised (like everything else in his life) with consummate grace and style. Now, with the Coronation approaching, the King had ambitions of being seen as the king of the whole nation, and imagined that being friends with politicians of both parties would foster this impression. Why anyone would imagine that politicians represent the nation I cannot think. They merely cling to it.

Matters in my apartment were on the surface decorous. Ann was about her business of brushing and scrubbing, and Davy was doing little jobs of repair and renovation. What had gone on while I was at Lord Hertford's I did not enquire into. I told Davy of the invitation, and we agreed I had to present my best front to the fashionable world. I showed him how to give my clothes their least threadbare aspect, and we discussed which of my jewels, walking-sticks and snuff boxes I should redeem from the pawnbrokers. The matter occupied me inordinately over the next few days, but Davy was eager to learn and I was pleased to teach, hoping it would keep his mind off his plight and off the opposite sex. I could see that my little maid was displeased with the amount of time I spent around the house, but of course there was nothing she could do about it.

Five days later I was getting ready for the party, dressing with unusual care, getting the inspiration for last-minute touches, practising postures and reverential attitudes before the looking-glass (if one is going to genuflect one should do so with grace). Lord Egremere had invited me as a guest, and I intended my behaviour and my air to be the equal of any of the other guests – nay, of Prinny himself. We both of us could show something to the present degenerate age. When I set off for Egremere

155

House I was seen off at the door by Davy, smiling delightedly and applauding in his artless way. The effect was spoiled by a street-urchin imitating my walk and tenue up and down the street in front of the expensively-hired carriage and horses. I could see the coachman was not impressed.

I had been to Egremere House before, but not for several years. In his young days Lord Egremere had been an enthusiastic member of the Benefice Lodge. That was when our brotherhood was the preserve of fiery and radical spirits, eager for progress and change and the brotherhood of man. That was when there were still aristocrats willing to subscribe to such ideals. Over the years the Lodge has been taken over by more conservative figures such as Lord Hertford, people who are not a whit attracted by the notion of the brotherhood of man, but seem to be more concerned with the giving or receiving of favours of a political or financial kind. Lord Egremere, though still going through the motions of membership, has largely dropped out. I, who am very much preoccupied with the receiving if not the giving of favours, remain very active. If self-interest is to be the new motive-force of society, I can be as self-interested as anybody.

The House had hardly changed since the days when the Lodge met there. It is even more splendid than Hertford House, as Whig aristocrats do seem to have the edge over Tory ones in the matter of wealth. Hertford House is splendid in a chilly kind of way, but at Egremere House you know that everything is quite simply the best of its kind, or was when it was acquired, and thus it has the unity of superb taste of various ages. It was clear from the carriages outside and the personages gathering on the pavement that this was to be an assembly of the notables of both political parties, and as we went up the superb marble staircase it was obvious that many of the noble guests were seeing the house for the first time. I heard the Duke of Wellington opine that it was a 'damned fine house', and say it was a pity that Egremere was 'not one of us'.

As we assembled in the magnificent first floor galleries

and rooms and made somewhat nervous talk over wonderful champagne (I'm sure it *was* wonderful, but I don't like the drink – my stomach makes extraordinarily unmusical noises after only a few sips, and my bowels are loosened for days), it became clear that everyone had arrived early so that the stage could be set for the Coming of Prinny. One who was clearly anticipating his coming somewhat nervously was Therese Hubermann-Cortino, the only other musician I could see at the party, who was to perform later.

'You will see, he will come with Lady Conyngham,' she whispered. 'Lord Egremere would be well advised to lock up his silver, but I suppose that is hardly practicable.'

I thought she looked discontented, and therefore less divine than usual. She was born to play not fire-spitting heroines such as Monsieur Cherubini's Medea but noble, yearning, wronged figures such as my Countess. Her forbidding bean-pole of a spouse was swapping tedious military yarns with the Victor of Waterloo a few feet away from us, so I felt that if social success was her ambition she had achieved it in full measure. By gently probing I elicited the cause of her discontent.

'I am here as a performer,' she said, with a little *moue*. 'Later on I am to cast my pearls before these swine. I should be here as a guest.'

I was not inclined to dispute her description of the other guests, but I did wonder why she thought it preferable to be one of the swine rather than an entertainer of swine. It has always been a wonder to me that people who wish to rise in aristocratic circles often express the utmost contempt for the people already in those circles. But I was prevented from saying anything because a hush slowly settled on the magnificent assembly.

Prinny had arrived.

The hush lasted a great while. I imagined Prinny heaving his Leviathantine bulk up that splendid staircase step by step, becoming redder and redder with the effort, and finally having to rest his once-beautiful but now inadequate legs at the top. But finally he made his entrance, Lord Egremere at his side. He was a sight to behold, ineffably condescending, dispensing graciousness

157

and bonhomie in a somewhat generalised way to all around him. I watched him, marvelling at his technique: how he took care to exchange words with both Whigs and Tories, brought them together by a gesture, flattered their women-folk. I wondered if the matter of his talk was as well-judged as the manner: after all, if he ever took notice of me it was morally certain that he would want to talk about Rossini.

Lord Hertford, as Lord Chamberlain, came in behind the King and remained close to him, as did his equine lady, harnessed in more diamonds than it had ever been my privilege to see on a single neck. If conspicuous display is vulgar, then Lady Hertford was a noble fish-wife. Also staying close to the King was a stout, puffy-faced woman with tiny eyes and an assertive manner who I knew to be Lady Conyngham. Between her and Lady Hertford there was a frosty politeness that you could have chilled the champagne with.

'Look at that greedy cow,' whispered Therese. 'She'd kill her own mother for half a sovereign.'

I must say I was shocked at the language of my idol.

Gradually the party began to loosen up. Prinny got around him an exquisitely-judged group of many political persuasions and he dispensed royal graciousness, not greatly helped by Lady Conyngham, who had by now contrived to get by his side. Lord Egremere mingled with his guests, a genial presence, and eventually came over to me and singled me out for special notice.

'Ah, Mr Mozart, honoured by your presence. I hear whispers that a new opera by you is indeed to be performed for the Coronation. That was a most prescient conversation we had on the day of the old King's death.'

Or alternatively the beginning of all my troubles. But I hastened to agree.

'It certainly was, My Lord. Yes, the opera is ready. I hope we shall begin rehearsals for it in the Spring.'

'Splendid. All the sordid financial details settled, eh?'

'I believe so. Lord Hertford is being most generous.'

'You're a lucky man. Because times are hard, and there is very little money around.'

That, being translated, meant: if he withdraws his offer,

158

don't come running to me.

'The country is certainly in a sad state,' I murmured. 'Though there seemed to be a lot of money around in the North, where I was recently.'

'Ah, the North. It's another country. It's from the North our salvation will come – and our liberation from this dreadful government, though I'm not supposed to be saying things like that tonight!'

He was giving me a roguish look when the King himself wobbled over, Lady Conyngham in his wake. As I bowed low towards the gargantuan paunch I wondered in what corslet of iron it could be encased so that he could present some kind of impressive figure at his own Coronation.

'Ah, Mr Mozart! Delighted to see you once more. I hear you are having a great success with *The Call to Arms.*'

'The public does seem pleased with it, Your Majesty.'

'Splendid. I shall certainly come and see it, when my engagements allow.'

'We will be honoured, sir.'

'Ah, we must show this Signor Rossini he's not the only one who can write a good tune, eh? I'm disappointed in the man. He threw away an opportunity that won't soon come again. But you'll show him with your new piece, eh, Mr Mozart? Eh, Mr Mozart?'

And he passed on, followed by the substantial shadow of Lady Conyngham.

'You have just been the victim of royal tact,' said Lord Egremere.

'I'm used to it,' I said. 'At Brighton I was told I could learn a lot from Signor Rossini. After that, to imply that we are competing in some kind of European tune contest is quite mild.'

Lord Egremere laughed.

'You know, I had thought to invite the Duke of Clarence tonight, as being the nearest thing to a royal Whig. But the thought of his rattling tactlessness made me forbear. It would have led to open warfare.' He turned as his shoulder was tapped by a superior flunky, who whispered in his ear. He turned back to me, consternation on his face. 'Dear me, Mr Mozart. Disaster threatens. The accompanist

159

to the wonderful Mme Hubermann-Cortino has fallen down drunk in the ante-room where he was waiting. But some accompanist she must have. I don't suppose you. . .'

I was mortified. It occurred to me that I had been invited as some kind of reserve player, with just this kind of emergency in mind.

'Delighted, My Lord,' I said.

There was no time for preparation or rehearsal. I was hurried with Therese to the back of the room where we had to step over the hack pianist stretched on the floor, snoring. Therese showed me the arias she intended to sing and I hadn't time to do more than register what they were when we heard Lord Egremere announcing (he did it very nicely) that there had been an emergency, but 'my honoured guest the great Mr Mozart' had very kindly stepped into the breach. Then we went out. I was back in my habitual role of public performer.

Therese had been asked to sing for fifteen or twenty minutes. She sang a piece of innocuous Pergolesi to warm up, then, 'Oh, had I Jubal's lyre' to satisfy the royal Handel-lust, the Willow Song from the charlatan of Pesaro's burlesque of *Othello*, and lastly 'Batti, batti', which she sang divinely as she did everything else. We managed one of Haydn's English songs as an encore, and then we were allowed to go. We were a mere interlude in the peace-making between the political parties. As we refreshed ourselves with glasses of good German wine from the only bottle the drunken accompanist had left untouched, Therese said:

'And that, I think, was my swan song in this accursed land!'

I looked at her, open-mouthed with consternation.

'Your swan song! But what about the opera season? The Coronation opera season?'

She shrugged.

'It will go on without me. Or it will not – no matter. I am going. My mission has failed.'

I was suspicious at once.

'Your mission? What was that? Was it something to do with the Queen?'

She smiled, not very divinely.

160

'You're really quite clever, Mr Mozart. That was not my mission, but I did have a *com*mission concerning the Queen. On our way to England we stopped off in my native Brunswick and talked to the reigning Duke. He was worried about the harm his mad aunt was doing to his country's reputation on the Continent, and I promised – for a consideration – to seek an audience with the Queen, with a view to persuading her to accept the King's offer of a pension if she agreed to return to Italy, or Turkey, or China, or wherever on earth she thought she might be happy.'

'With no success, alas.'

'None whatever. The moment we met I realised the woman is drunk on public acclamation. She talks of nothing but the deputations and loyal addresses she has received, the deafening cheers that greet her in the streets. She is drugged with acclaim. I have seen that in opera singers. I recognise it.'

'But your commission enabled you to take news of it to the King,' I suggested, my eyes now well open to the woman (how had I been so blind? Because she was a woman, and a German woman?).

'Clever again, Mr Mozart. Which was of course from the first our object in coming here.'

'Why? Do you collect royalty?'

She tweaked my nose.

'In a way. I see you are bewildered, dear, innocent Mr Mozart. Royal personages, let me tell you, are not more cultured or witty than other souls. Certainly they are not more generous. You of all people, will know that. But what you may not know is that at the end of an affair with royalty the pay-off is superb because all the royal family and all the flunky politicians around them are so anxious to avoid a scandal. All they are worried about is that you do not take your story to the public prints. A hundred years ago – fifty – it would not have been so, but to be royal, in the nineteenth century, is to be bourgeois. They have to pretend to be like their subjects, so that their subjects will love them as they love themselves.'

'Prinny doesn't pretend to be like his subjects.'

'No. That is probably why he is so unpopular. He is a

figure from a previous era. Prinny was a bad choice. My husband and I agree: in future we will research our projects very much better. But that was not why I failed.'

'Oh?'

Her expression was bitter.

'There has been no affair because your King prefers old women to young ones, ugly women to beautiful ones. There has been no affair because the King probably doesn't do it any more. There has been no affair because your King probably can't find it any more. He'd probably have to send down a team of mountain climbers to find it, and how would you position yourself to receive the royal gift?' She saw I was shocked, and laughed vulgarly. 'So I'm off to look for better prospects. Someone who wants a mistress not a mother. It's been suggested that Sweden could be interested – a soldier of Napoleon, with whom my dear husband would have a lot in common. And Holland is dull, boorish but very rich. We shall do our preliminary reconnaissance among the crowned heads better this time.'

'But my—'

'But your opera. The Countess in *Figaro*. Alas, Mr Mozart, I shall have to deny myself the pleasure of singing your charming if now decidedly old-fashioned music. Try the Ackroyd girl: she has talent and seems to think you're the latest thing. You won't find many that think that these days. Try not to remember me unkindly: every woman, in this world that is cruel to women, has to put herself first, last, and all places in between. *Così*, as you would say, *Fan Tutte*. So let us go back to the party and *goodbye*, dear Mr Mozart.'

Stepping over the drunken accompanist I followed her out, dazed and grieved. My hopes for the opera season had been dealt a terrible blow. The little edifice I had been building since the late King's death seemed to be collapsing round me. The dreadful prospect opened up of an opera season *without* an opera of mine.

Back in the galleries and salons the party was going on famously well. How would it not, with so much graciousness on one side, so much fawning and flattery on the other. Where the King was, admiration and gratitude reigned, where he was not his words were being repeated from mouth to mouth, though without the *manner* they were hardly worth the saying, let alone repeating. I was about to close in on someone with good will, large unencumbered estates and a love of music when I saw something at the end of the Long Gallery.

One of the grandest of the footmen had come up to Lord Hertford. In his braided, be-gilt state as Lord Chamberlain he was unmistakable. A salver was presented, and Lord Hertford took from it some kind of note or small package. He found himself an unfrequented corner and opened it. Then he opened a further enclosure, and took out a note. Already I was nervous with anticipation. It took him no more than a second to read. Then he began back towards the throng, his eyes going everywhere.

Who else could he be looking for but me?

I thought of slipping away, but what I evaded tonight would catch up with me tomorrow. This damned business was like a chain on my leg, and it would never be removed until it was solved or settled. I began making my way in Lord Hertford's direction.

'Ah, Mr Mozart!' he said, *sotto voce.*

He pulled me a little aside and handed me a roughly-torn sheet of paper. The note, written in a firm, educated hand, read:

'What I want is a thousand guineas. Have it ready by Monday.'

I gazed at it in search of a clue, but found none. A man or a strong-minded woman with a love of money – that again about summed it up. Then I turned the page and found my clue.

The paper I use in my jakes is always unwanted off-prints from publishers. Preferably novels, because I sometimes sit there contentedly reading. The rough bundle of sheets there at that moment was of a reprint of that old favourite *A Gentleman of Quality.* It had given me pleasure to think that I was wiping my arse on a gentleman of quality. I knew that that morning I had reached the end of the first volume.

Turning the note over I saw the title page of the second volume.

163

CHAPTER SEVENTEEN
Sono in Trappola

I walked back home more uneasy and uncertain than I had ever been. When I had read the note and marshalled my composure I had said to Lord Hertford merely that this second note needed to be thought over, and that I would communicate my thoughts the next day. I could have communicated them then, though I chose not to: they were that Davy had used my partial communication of what happened on the night of Jenny's death to launch a crude and dangerous blackmail attempt. I had been as mistaken in my estimate of his character as I had been about that of Mme Hubermann-Cortino: simple and endearing he was, but he had a most defective moral code. It was clear that the prospect of easy money had sent him entirely off-balance.

Whether Lord Hertford had seen anything in my face as I read the note I did not know. I had been too confused and astonished to look him in the face. What I did know, alas, was that that wily old political schemer was as adept at reading people's thoughts as anyone in the world.

I was earlier home than I had expected to be or told Davy I would be, and I was relieved to find there was no evidence of Ann in the apartment. Davy heard my key in the door and as I came into my sitting-room he emerged from his bedroom, still in shirt and breeches, smiling and welcoming.

'Did it go well, Mr Mozart? Was it a right-down good party?'

'It was, in a way, Davy,' I said, my face giving nothing

away. 'Sit down and we'll talk about it. I think we need a little more light, don't you? . . . There. And I think I need something to drink. Champagne does not really agree with me.'

'Champagne! That's a real swank drink, isn't it?'

'It is. Perhaps people who are used to it develop a stomach for it. I would infinitely rather have a good German wine, or even a good German beer. But let us have a glass of brandy, as we did the night you came here.'

I poured two glasses, and diluted them with water. He was sitting on the sofa, and I went and sat where I could see his face, that face of a guileless peasant, I had thought.

'Oh, what have you done, Davy?' I asked. His eyes opened wide, and he looked at me with that ingenuousness I had always liked.

'Done, Mr Mozart? I haven't done anything. Just little jobs while you've been out.'

I shook my head, infinitely sad: ingenuousness could be faked, like any other human quality.

'Oh, Davy, you've done much worse than that. Unless by "little jobs" you mean get somebody to write a letter to Lord Hertford demanding money.'

There was silence, and he looked down at his lap.

'Didn't think as they'd show you the note, Mr Mozart.'

'Didn't you?'

'Didn't think as you was so thick wi' the likes of them.'

I looked at him pityingly, the veil now removed from my eyes.

'My living depends on "the likes of them", Davy. In a crisis I am bound to do what they demand of me. I suppose I should be grateful you didn't use music paper, which was probably the only other sort you could find.'

'Didn't think that would be right . . . But it's a tip-top scheme, Mr Mozart!'

'It's a wicked scheme, Davy.'

'It is not. When you think what they did with my Jenny! Even a dog deserves a better end! He should pay for it, that Lord Hertford, and he will. You and I could be in it together, Mr Mozart. Go halves. We wouldn't put the screws on too often. Just enough to live comfortable, like.'

I took a big draught of brandy, trying not to get angry. I had to tell myself the boy was poor and ignorant.

'Davy, I am not a criminal, not a sharper, not a blackmailer. I am a respectable musician, far, far removed from that sort of person and his activities.'

'Then you seem to have got involved in some downright funny business!'

I swallowed.

'Very well. My judgment is not always what it should be, I admit that. Including my judgment of you . . . Very well, if I can't convince you of the immorality of your scheme, let me try to convince you of the folly of it.'

'Nay, it was a clever plan.'

'And the *danger* of it.'

'I can take care of myself.'

He squared his shoulders, as if taking on the world.

'Davy, in your ordinary sphere of life I have no doubt you can. But I've told you before: you have no idea of the resources of a man like Lord Hertford. If you cross him, he can have you rotting away the rest of your life in a filthy prison. He can have you transported. He can have you hanged. Or, what is even more likely, he can have you done away with quietly. What is more he *would*. I wouldn't give a ha'penny for your life if he found out you were trying to blackmail him.'

'Nay, you're exaggerating, Mr Mozart. Together we can put it over him.'

I took a deep breath.

'There is no question of "together", Davy. I would never get involved in a wicked plot like that.'

'Then perhaps you should, Mr Mozart. Going by what I hear from you you've knocked at their doors for handouts often enough. All your dignity as a respectable musician hasn't stopped you doing that, has it? A plan like mine has a lot more dignity to it, to my way of thinking – aye, and independence too. And there's a lot more to be got out of him in future, I'd guess.'

'Criminal folly has no dignity or independence to it, Davy. And folly it was. Who did you get to write your note for you? How do you know you could trust him? There's no trust among thieves, you know.'

He looked up at me, and as he did so an extremely unpleasant smile spread over his face. I was seized by foreboding. The voice that had spoken Davy's last speech had not been the voice of the Davy I knew. The Davy who smiled this smile was a hundred miles from the Davy I knew. I – *I*, so old in the ways of the theatre! – had been gulled by a performance, by an impersonation, similar to that Lord Hertford had been planning to put on for the benefit of the House of Lords.

'Oh, Mr Mozart,' this new Davy said, in this new voice that was not the voice of a yokel, 'you think me such a bumpkin, don't you? The boy from the country who can hardly spell out simple words.'

'You told me—'

He laughed unpleasantly.

'Oh, you don't want to believe everything I told you, Mr Mozart. There's no honour among thieves, as you said.'

'I am *not* a thief.'

'A borrower, though, who never repays unless forced. We have more than you think in common. And I can read and write with my betters. I went to the grammar school in Colchester. They beat Latin into me, and a bit of Greek. More than Shakespeare had, if what they say about him is true. Oh, I got an education all right, back there in Essex!'

'You should go back there – out of danger and harm's way.'

He stretched himself lazily.

'Now that wouldn't be convenient, Mr Mozart. The fact is, there was an agreement between me and a certain clergyman, the details of which I needn't go into. But the upshot was that for a price I agreed to stay away from Colchester, for the length of his lifetime.'

'You disgust me! You are a hardened criminal!'

'Wise to the ways of the world, more like.'

'You have deceived me entirely.'

'And yet if you'd thought, you might have had your suspicions, you know. Did it never seem odd to you that a bright, nice-looking, well-set-up lad like me should have as his sweetheart a snivelling little wretch like Jenny? Didn't it

167

ever occur to you that I could have done a lot better?'

'I didn't even think of it.'

The laziness left the body as he leaned forward tensely.

'No, because you regarded us as yokels and servants and outdoor labourers and you thought we didn't run our lives by the same sort of rules that you and your kind go by. You were above noticing our private affairs, weren't you?'

'I was very sorry for you when I thought you were in danger, God help me.'

He ignored this, to harp on his grievance.

'I'd be sorry for myself if I couldn't have done better for myself than *Jenny*!'

'You disgust me. You simply used her.'

'She was the one who had the information, so she was the one I used.'

'How did you come to assume this role as gardener's boy?'

He looked at me, smiling, wondering whether to tell. In the end his conceit made him, and he told it to bear witness to his own cleverness and resourcefulness, knowing that he had involved me so deeply his secrets were safe with me.

'Well, Mr Mozart, when I came to London last summer, in consequence of this agreement with the reverend gentleman, I was on the look out for where things were happening. Because where they were happening was where the opportunities for a bright young chap like me were. And what was happening was that the Queen was coming back, and the King was wild to rid himself of her. Well, I thought, there was no way I could get close to the King—'

'Unusually modest of you.'

'Don't get sarcastic with me, Mr Mozart!' he said sharply. 'You'd regret it. Well, the talk was that the Queen would be staying at Alderman Wood's until she could get somewhere suitable of her own. Now that seemed more promising. So I sniffed around, found that they'd improved the house no end in the hopes of having her lodge there, and were just starting to do similar to the garden. So I put on my Essex accent, dressed rough, and

168

went along looking simple and willing, and it worked like a charm.'

'I'm not surprised,' I said bitterly. 'It worked on me.'

'Oh, you were a pushover compared to Alderman Wood's head gardener. Once I'd started work I wormed my way into the house as much as I could: charmed cups of tea out of Cook, chatted to the maids and bedded them one by one in the garden at night. They all knew they were to come to me with anything they could learn about the Queen.'

I couldn't forbear asking, in spite of the repellent nature of his tale, what I had for so long itched to know: 'So the stories about the Queen weren't just made up?'

"Course they weren't. True in every respect – that was their strength. Jenny was going back in after a session with me in the garden that should have made her grateful to me for life – stupid cow! – and she heard everything she said she heard. Not that she understood all of it: I had to explain a lot next day, and even then I don't think she really *understood*. She had the brains of a rabbit.'

Poor, frightened, ignorant, despised Jenny!

'She did, I'm afraid, poor creature. If you'd been wise you'd have said you overheard all this yourself.'

'I know!' He banged his forehead. 'I'm a damned fool! But the reason I didn't was that it sounded so much better coming from a simple girl than from a man. I thought she'd just have to tell her story once, or twice at most. The possibility of her having to tell it to the House of Lords never occurred to me. Absurd thought! Impossible! As for me, I'd have enjoyed it. But the other thing was, I didn't want my background investigated. There are things there that, as soon as I was named, could have come out. So I preferred to remain as a sort of honest bystander.'

'How did you get the information to Lord Hertford? That's something I've never heard the details of.'

'We sent him a note. Jenny wrote at my dictation – she took hours! He was to reply to a stationer's in the vicinity. Naturally I'd heard of Lord Hertford as the King's cuckold. Anyway, we didn't hurry things. We didn't write till some weeks after the Queen's stay at Alderman

Wood's: I was happy to give the impression that we were slow, rather stupid folk. By then I'd promised Jenny marriage – said we'd get the money out of Lord Hertford and set up a business, maybe a tavern, somewhere.'

'Which you *wouldn't* have done, I take it?'

He smiled his unpleasant smile of male pride.

'Ha! Set up anything with Jenny? Small chance! I'd have used it as I shall use what I get out of Lord Hertford now: to rise in the world. You don't rise from a tavern.'

'Not often.'

'Anyway, the notes went backwards and forwards to Mr de Fries – you know Mr de Fries?—'

'Yes, I know him.'

'Probably hands over His Lordship's meagre gifts to you now and then, does he? Well, the notes took more time, I got them interested, then finally I took Jenny by appointment to Hertford House and left her there. Goodness she was in a shake! After that – well, you know about the next few weeks.'

'Not about you and her. I only know what you told me about that.'

He smiled sardonically. He was feeling very superior to me.

'Well, of course what I told you wasn't entirely true. You're not as sharp in the ways of the world as you think you are, Mr Mozart. I got a note from her after she'd only been in the theatre a night or two. It was one of those who wait around in the Haymarket who brought it. I'd never have been able to decipher it if I hadn't got so used to her horrible scrawl. That night I was on watch there, and about midnight she let me in. After that I was there every night. It was better than sleeping with Sam the gardener's boy at Simon Mullins's – just! She was such a bore.'

'And you are such a cad.'

He bent forward in mock deference, then handed me his glass to refill.

'I take your word for it, Mr Mozart – from one who has mixed in gentlemanly circles. Oh, but she was such a bore. The first few nights I heard nothing but how frightened she was. Over and over she said it: "I'm so frightened." I

170

kept pressing her for details of what Lord Hertford had promised, and she said he'd promised to set us up in business. I kept telling her to insist we wanted cash or there was no deal, and she'd go on again about how frightened she was, and how could she *insist* to someone like that? Then, after a bit, a change came over her . . .'

'Oh? Did she go off you?'

He shook his head pityingly.

'Not a bit. She was besotted. No, the change was that she got less frightened. I was pleased for a bit, since she'd got on my nerves. I thought she was acquiring a bit of confidence, which was fine. Then she let slip that she might not have to testify before the House of Lords.'

'I don't see why that should worry you.'

He looked aggravated by my slowness.

'Oh, Mr Mozart, you really don't understand, do you? The bigger the service she did His Lordship, the more we had on him and the bigger the claim we could make. I'd have reckoned on at least a thousand.'

'You seem to like that nice round sum.'

His tongue flicked round his lips.

'I do. I regard it as a stepping stone to ten thousand. Anyway, when I got it out of her what was actually proposed I was livid. If that was what was going to happen, the bulk would go to this Ackroyd whore, and he'd be paying us off with fifty guineas. That's how noblemen work.'

'Yes,' I said; 'that's how noblemen work.'

'You see?' he said, excited and angry. 'You *know*, but you don't fight it. They walk all over the likes of you. Anyway that was two days before . . . before she was killed. I really exploded, I can tell you. I told her if this went ahead we'd lose everything – be thrown aside like a glove with a hole in it. I told her she had to tell Mr de Fries that he couldn't do that: that unless it was she who went and testified at the trial she'd expose the impersonation.'

'That could have been dangerous.'

'Not for me. Anyway, the next night came. She had no guile – couldn't lie. Can you imagine, not being able to lie? Just like an animal. She admitted she hadn't done it. This time I had to use a bit of physical persuasion. By the time I was done with her she'd promised to do it.'

'I suppose you're proud?'

'No I'm not, because it didn't work. The next night I was on tenterhooks. I couldn't wait. I had to know if she'd done it. That was that special night at the theatre – lots of nobs, and all in their finest. I watched, thinking one day I'd be among them. But like I say I was getting desperate. After the interval I slipped through the stage door—'

'*You* came in?' I said, knowing in my heart what was coming.

'Oh yes,' he said, with his superior smile. 'No problem to that. The keeper often went to see the play during the later parts of the pieces – I knew that by watching, and by what Jenny told me. By then the Queen's was a second home to me. I ran up the stairs and made it to the Ackroyd cow's dressing-room. Jenny was there, just sitting, her hands tearing at a wet handkerchief. Just seeing her I knew she hadn't done it. She got up and ran over to me, crying stuff about she *couldn't*, and she was sure there was another way, and I was so clever I could surely find it. I was mad with rage. I took out the pruning knife I had on me—'

'You came meaning to kill her!'

'Not me. I carried that knife all the time. You need a weapon in London. She was clinging to me. My eyes seemed to be swimming in blood. I plunged it into her, and then again. The next thing I knew she was lying at my feet.'

I couldn't think of anything to say. A minute ticked by. Finally I said: 'You monster. You murderer.' Even as I said it, it sounded not merely feeble but ridiculous.

'The girl was a ball and chain on my leg,' he said, shrugging, not a trace of compunction on his face. 'She was no use to me by then. We'd had the chance of making a thousand, and she'd thrown it away. I had to free myself of her.'

'Why didn't you run for it when you'd killed her?'

'I did. I got out of that theatre and then ran across Haymarket and into the backstreets. Then suddenly I

172

thought: why am I running? I'm not an obvious suspect. I ought to go back there and see what happens. And when the play ended, the audience went home, then the actors, and nothing *did* happen – well then, Mr Mozart, I really started thinking.'

'And when you saw the body being removed, you knew. And all you could think of was the opportunities for blackmail.'

'Right! I'd done something stupid and unnecessary, out of pure rage, but I'd been given the chance of getting into something even better. Something really juicy! Someone up there likes me, that's certain. Oh dear, I laughed inside when you spun me that tale of removing properties from theatre to theatre. You must have thought me a booby!'

'You were playing a booby!'

He agreed complacently.

'I was. I've known enough of them in my time. And it paid off. You played right into my hands. As soon as you said Jenny had probably gone to another theatre I knew the death was being covered up.' He eyed me craftily. 'And as soon as you warned me I might be in danger I knew your fate and mine were intertwined.'

'They are not!'

He shook his head confidently.

'Oh but they are, Mr Mozart. You've been concealing a murderer and a blackmailer in your apartment for the last three weeks and more. How is that going to look to the authorities? How is it going to look to Lord Hertford?'

'I was duped. There is no shame in being duped.'

He laughed scornfully.

'You think not? *I'd* be ashamed of being such a gull. And Lord Hertford is at the very least going to be very unimpressed. What are you hoping for from him at the moment? You must be hoping for *something*, to let yourself get involved with his schemes as you have done. What is it? Support for your new opera?'

'Well—'

'Ah, that's it. Well, the world mustn't be denied a new opera by Mr Mozart, must it? If I were you I'd do my best to keep in his favour. And you won't do that by admitting that you've been concealing Jenny's murderer in your living quarters – particularly if Lord Hertford realises that what you were hiding him from was assassination by a gang of bravos hired by His Lordship himself. That was what you feared, wasn't it?'

The boy was so sharp! He had understood my every move. I nodded miserably.

'I thought that, when you first warned me of danger. There you are, then: your credit with His Lordship is gone for ever. Now, I suggest you've got two possibilities.' He leaned forward, as if explaining to a backward child. 'The first is that you keep quiet about what I'm up to and let me get on with it. That way you keep your lily-white hands clean, or as clean as possible. It's a fine thing to have a clear conscience, I'm sure of that.' He laughed sardonically, and got down on his haunches in front of me, his evil face inches from mine, looking me in the eye. 'But the second alternative is what you'll choose if you've an ounce of brains or gumption. You come in this with me – and not just this, but any similar scheme in the future. Your connections and your knowledge of the nobs, even the royals, will be invaluable to me. We'd make a fine team. And you could teach me things – etiquette, forms of address, how to mingle with my betters like you've done. I'll learn fast – you'll admit I'm a fast learner?'

'Oh yes,' I said sadly. 'Quick as lightning.'

'There you are then. You'll rake money in – far more than you have done fawning on the nobs and gentry for free hand-outs. You'll be living on your wits, which is how *Homo sapiens* should live. And you could still write your music: you'd have plenty of time for that. Now, what do you say, Mr Mozart? Will you come into partnership with me?'

There was a long, long silence. I was not – do me that justice, dear reader – considering whether to go into partnership with this horrible boy. The thought never crossed my mind. I was thinking over what to do. I had never met his like before: the human creature who is totally devoid of moral sense. I have known criminals, but they have always had a dim understanding of the moral

174

code they are violating. I have known libertines and wastrels – men such as my dear old friend da Ponte – who scorn the moral code of ordinary humanity but construct a new morality for themselves which allows them to do what they do, even approves it as right and admirable. But where a moral sense should be in this lad there was a blank, a terrible blackness. No code of right or wrong – not the Turk's, the Chinaman's nor the Red Indian's – would mean anything to him. He was a moral void.

And he had murdered – quite casually, senselessly, because the woman he was using as a tool would not do his will. As I saw it he had killed her to assert his dominance over her. That being so, he could go on and do it again – and perhaps again and again. There was a terrible responsibility on me. At last I spoke.

'I cannot at my age become a criminal,' I said. 'It is too late. I choose your first alternative.'

'Very well,' said Davy, getting up from his haunches. 'You're a fool, but so be it. But you agree to be silent as the grave and let me get on with it?'

'I do. I have little choice. In any case your crimes are your own affair. But you cannot go on committing them from this apartment. That would be too dangerous for you as well as for me. People will be coming here the whole time, including men in Lord Hertford's employ.' That was a lie. Few people came to my apartment except musicians and actors, and occasionally Mrs Sackville from Frith Street. 'You will have to get out, and get out now, under cover of night.'

'That suits me,' said Davy, looking around him contemptuously. 'I'll be getting a lot better quarters than this in no time. Well, I'm sorry to lose you as a partner, Mr Mozart, but not sorry to have the scheme all to myself. I anticipate being nicely in funds before another week has passed. Ah well: easy come, easy go. I'll get my jacket, get my few little things, and be on my way. I've enjoyed my time here. Very comfortable and civilised, even if not grand. I can weather a night on the streets tonight, and after that there's plenty of beds I can go to – old Simon Mullins's if I'm really pressed.'

He had gone into his little bedroom, put on his jacket,

and was filling the pockets with his few possessions. My heart stopped when I saw that one of them was a lethal-looking pruning knife. I have never felt so vulnerable in my own place. He was soon ready, and came over. He did not pull out the knife, but I was very conscious which pocket it was in.

'I'm not going to threaten you, Mr Mozart,' he said, with a chilling smile. 'You're too lily-livered to do anything brave – and crossing me would *really* be brave, wouldn't it? Goodbye. Enjoy the rest of your life, kowtowing to the rich and titled. Remember you've got more genius in your little finger than they have in their whole bodies. I have too – and I'll be using it to get up there with them!'

I could not bear to look up at him. He crossed to the door, I heard it slam, and then his footsteps going down the stairs two at a time. I rose and locked the door, keeping his terrible presence at bay, keeping the *feel* of his evil nature out. Then I went back and sat for a long time in the lamp- and candle-light. This had been a long and terrible night – the most terrible since my dear father died. But I felt that I had to end it by doing something, by making a decision and acting on it. At last I went to my desk. I was annoyed to find only music paper there. I tore off a bit of blank paper at the top of one of the sheets and wrote:

My Lord,

I have made some investigations, and I conclude that Your Lordship will be quite safe in ignoring any demands from the quarter we know of. I believe that the one who makes the demands was the perpetrator of the deed.

I hear that the boy Davy House is back on the London streets, and may perhaps be found in the vicinity of Dover Street, possibly at the house of Simon Mullins.

I have the honour to be
Your Lordship's humble servant
Wolfgang Gottlieb Mozart

I sealed it. Then I went to bed, but not to sleep.

CHAPTER EIGHTEEN
Rondo Finale

I sent my note to Lord Hertford with a heavy heart. I also sent one to the theatre saying I had a bad cold and would not be directing any performances for some days. I took to my bed on the first day, as a token, but Ann would not have noticed what I did: she was too taken up with grieving at the departure of Davy House. I told her he had gone to try his fortunes up North.

Meanwhile I sketched the principal themes of a new piano concerto, and then began to compose in earnest. A new libretto arrived from Edward Clarkson, as usual with a summary of the story (he knew I wouldn't bother to read it). It was called *Victor and Victoria* – a sign that the public imagination is beginning to be exercised by the little Princess in Kensington Palace. Over meals I read the feeble words to the airs and jotted down suitably innocuous tunes. I was not unhappy, particularly as I had the last novel of the late Miss Austen to read.

I stayed in my apartment for ten days. When I was bored from want of occupation I wrote a few eleemosynary letters for future use, just to keep my hand in. When at last I went to the theatre I took a carriage there and back. I rehearsed the company, put some energy and discipline back into the performances, then I went home. I wished I knew if I was safe from the murderous impulses of Davy House, but this was hardly something I could bring up with Lord Hertford or Mr de Fries.

Gradually however I regained confidence. I walked to the theatre and to my usual taverns and eating houses. I still had the greater part of Lord Hertford's eighty guineas, and Mr Novello had paid me generously for my 105th symphony. I had money to spend, and I spent it. I agreed to go to my daughter Theresa in Canterbury for Christmas, though I find the English celebrations of that holy and joyful time pallid and lifeless compared to those that take place in my dear German homeland.

My life was returning to normal.

It was nearly a month after I had ejected Davy from my life that I had any sort of conversation with Mr Popper. Conversation with Mr Popper is something I normally avoid, but a talk about the forthcoming opera season was becoming a necessity. I had the impression that decisions were being taken, arrangements made, that I had not been consulted about, or even informed of. I had some time to spare after a rehearsal and I dropped into his office to tell him that I had finished composing the airs to *Victor and Victoria*. He gave every sign of being optimistic for its success.

'Capital, capital!' he said, rubbing his hands. 'We must build on the success of *The Call to Arms*. We could have it on stage by February. Is it an attractive story?'

I shrugged.

'I have no idea. As attractive as usual, I suppose.'

'You will have your fun, Mr Mozart.' He cleared his throat. 'Well, well, things seem to be going well now, after our little difficulties.'

'They do?'

'Oh yes. Lord Hertford tells me that he is sure any problems in connection with *that unfortunate matter* are at an end.'

'I see.' And I did see, and – God forgive me – I was relieved. 'But the problems of the opera season—'

'Problems, Mr Mozart?'

'The departure of Mme Hubermann-Cortino.'

'Solved, my dear sir! I had a letter only yesterday from Mme Pizzicoli. She says she is delighted to hear that the prejudices of the English against her fellow countrymen have abated, and she will be delighted to travel here to sing in the Coronation opera season.'

178

'The woman is a bird-brain.'

'Since when has that harmed a prima donna?' Mr Popper asked, quite reasonably. 'I have written offering her very generous terms. I shall write to Mme Ardizzi too, renewing my offer.'

'I see,' I said, foreseeing struggles ahead. 'I imagine each of the ladies will require a special production centred around herself.'

'They will. They always do. Mme Pizzicoli mentions *The Barber of Seville*. That should present no problems. If we have to do *La Vestale* for Mme Ardizzi, so be it. A few Roman columns and a lot of nightdresses should do the trick.'

I coughed.

'Mme Hubermann-Cortino was to sing my Countess.'

Mr Popper gazed at the floor. I caught the sound of feet shuffling on bare floor-boards.

'Ah yes. Sad for you. Still, water under the bridge. . .'

'What do you mean?'

He looked up, gazing into my eyes with managerial shamelessness.

'Well, Mr Mozart, the production of *Figaro* was to be a special tribute to the genius of Mme Hubermann-Cortino, as you well know. Without her there would be no point.'

'No point!'

'Lord Hertford, alas, is having to be a little careful at the moment. Someone has alerted Lady Hertford to the money he is spending on the season. Quite apart from . . . anything else.'

My heart sank.

'Anything else?'

There was the sound of shoe leather on the floor-boards again.

'Oh, just an impression, Mr Mozart.'

'*What* impression, Mr Popper?'

'Just an impression that you're not entirely popular with Lord Hertford at the moment.'

That completed my discomfiture. My worst suspicions were confirmed, and I had only myself to blame: I had written to Lady Hertford, I had shielded Davy House.

'Has any . . . reason been given for this, Mr Popper?'

'None at all,' he said airily. 'It hasn't been discussed. It's just an impression as I say.'

I knew why I was not popular. Lord Hertford had made the right connection that I had intended him to make in my note – that the blackmail attempt was the work of Davy House – and he had acted accordingly. But he had made another connection too: that until I had realised what he was up to I had been hiding Davy. The fact that he was right about this too did not lessen the blow. I had no doubt I had given the game away by my reaction to Davy's note. By my lack of guile, and by my terrible misjudgments of people, I had ruined the chances of my lovely old opera.

'But then there's the question of the new opera,' I said.

'Ah, well, yes. We'll certainly hope to do something with that,' said Popper, palpably not re-emerging from his shuffling phase.

'*Hope?*'

'Much will depend on the public, of course. Will the favour they have shown *The Call to Arms* spill over on to a new full-length work by you?'

'The two pieces shouldn't be mentioned in the same breath!' I protested.

'Ah, I can understand your feelings,' lied Mr Popper. 'But remember I haven't seen anything of the new piece. And your operas have not always been to the taste of the British public.'

'They loved *The Enchanted Violin*.'

'They did,' conceded Popper.

'And they'll love this one too. I have at last found the right title for it.'

'You have?' said Popper without interest.

'Yes. All the ones I've toyed with were too long and lacking in bite. I shall call it *Falstaff*.'

There was a semi-breve of silence.

'You will call it *what?*'

'*Falstaff*. It came to me when I was sick. I know it's been used by dear old Salieri, but his is not a piece anyone plays any more. It's much better than any of the ones I've been toying with.'

'Am I to take it,' asked Mr Popper, at his most absurdly

180

pompous, 'that this new opera of yours deals with Sir John Falstaff?'

'Of course it does,' I said in astonishment. 'You've heard all the translations I've been trying of *The Merry Wives of Windsor.*'

'You don't imagine I understand Italian, do you, Mr Mozart?'

'I thought you might understand "Windsor".'

'Not when you pronounce it "Weeensor".' He drew himself up to his full five foot five. 'Well, I must say I'm surprised at you, Mr Mozart.'

'Surprised?'

'That you could have thought of inflicting such an opera on me for the Coronation season.'

'But you haven't heard a note of it!'

'I don't need to. The mere fact of the central figure being a grotesquely fat and bibulous man is enough to tell me it is entirely unsuitable. The fact that it is a play where he tries to make love to a variety of women at the same time makes it totally impossible. The public would take it as a deliberate insult to the King. The Merry Wives of *Windsor* – the King's principal home! Either they would be shocked or they would be delighted. In either case royal patronage of the season would be out of the question.'

I looked at him in dumbfounded consternation. I had never for a moment thought of that. For once in his inglorious life Mr Popper was right.

'So all my hopes for my new opera. . .'

'Dead, Mr Mozart.' He said it with horrible satisfaction. 'And you have only yourself to blame. We shall have to think of something else. That's a decision I shall take out of your hands. As a foreigner you obviously have no idea what is suitable. I will talk to Mr Clarkson. Off the cuff I would say that *Il Matrimonio Segreto* would be ideal. Charming little piece, very easy on the ear, not too heavy, unlike . . . Good day, Mr Mozart.'

And he bustled off.

I turned and walked out of the theatre. I felt I had to drag my limbs as I began the walk to Henrietta Street. My whole world was shattered. All the hopes and expectations

181

I had been building for my entrancing new opera had been rudely demolished. I felt a total distaste for the opera house, for opera managers and all their works. Mr Popper may have been right about the unsuitability of *Falstaff* as a subject for Coronation year, but he had just been looking for an excuse. If not that it would have been some other. I had toiled for him for years, directing rubbish, composing meretricious pieces to words beneath contempt, only at the end of my life to be treated worse than a cleaner or a doorman. My dreams for *Falstaff* were over. It would never be performed. Probably the good Mr Novello would not even be interested in publishing it.

I decided this was the end. I probably had only a few years left in me, but I certainly did not want to spend them in the opera house. I would retire, go and live in the North, with my son, or near him. In the North I was appreciated. The North was wonderfully cheap. I could live by my music there, as I could not in fashionable London.

If only they wouldn't keep mentioning *Messiah*. . .

But I could put up with that, because up there I would be surrounded by musical people, people who appreciated me. And up North there was not an opera house to be found. I would be free at last. I could shake the dust of opera houses from my feet for ever.

Probably.

Because a thought occurred to me. Mr Popper was quite right about *Il Matrimonio Segreto*: it is the sort of light, insubstantial piece that would be suitable for a Coronation season. Except for one thing: the subject of a clandestine marriage was an even worse subject to play before the King than mine of a bibulous, amorous glutton. The King's early and secret marriage to Mrs Fitzherbert, that good and much-wronged lady, had dogged him for years. That was why his subjects still shouted 'Mr Fitzherbert' at him.

Mr Popper's lack of Italian had let him down again.

And if Mr Popper went ahead with his plan, got his cast together, and then, if, just before the season someone (me, if necessary, but I could probably arrange for someone else to do it) should point out to him the impossibility of this particular subject, then I could step in with my *Figaro*. Not *Don Giovanni* (unsuitable subject yet again!) but *Figaro*. Or even that wonderful yet economical piece *Così* – that divine piece that the cloth-eared English stayed away from in droves when it was first produced.

My steps became lighter. I looked round at passing Londoners, at bankers and whores, noblemen and thieves, and I smiled on them in anticipation of a delightful manoeuvre, skillfully executed, leading to one of my *real* pieces reaching the stage again.

By the time I reached home I was infused with that lunatic optimism which, against all likelihood, against all experience, against all reason, buoys up those who are condemned to spend a life sentence working in the opera house.